U l

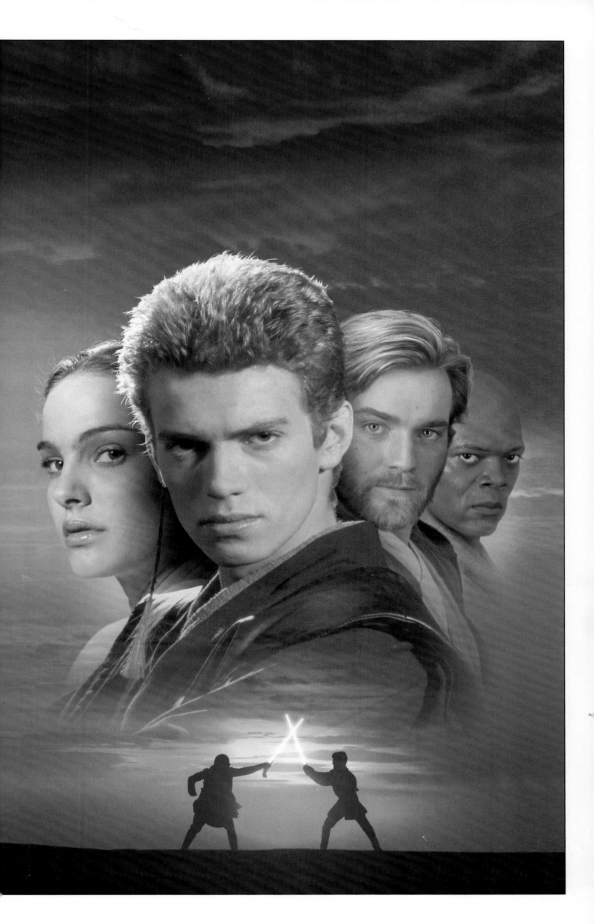

STAR WARS®

EPISODE II

ATTACK OF THE CLONES™

VOLUME ONE

ADAPTED BY
HENRY GILROY

BASED ON THE ORIGINAL STORY BY
GEORGE LUCAS

AND THE SCREENPLAY BY
GEORGE LUCAS AND
JONATHAN HALES

PENCILS
JAN DUURSEMA

INKS
RAY KRYSSING

COLORS
DAVE MCCAIG

COLOR SEPARATOR
HAROLD MACKINNON

LETTERS
STEVE DUTRO

COVER ART
TSUNEO SANDA

DARK HORSE COMICS

Spotlight

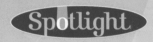

VISIT US AT
www.abdopublishing.com

einforced library bound edition published in 2009 by Spotlight, a division of the ABDO Group, 8000 Vest 78th Street, Edina, Minnesota 55439. Spotlight produces high-quality reinforced library bound ditions for schools and libraries. Published by agreement with Dark Horse Comics, Inc., and ucasfilm Ltd.

Library of Congress Cataloging-in-Publication Data

ilroy, Henry.
Episode II : attack of the clones / story, George Lucas ; script, Henry Gilroy ;
encils, Jan Duursema ; inks, Ray Kryssing ; colors, Dave McCaig ; letters, Steve
utro. -- Reinforced library bound ed.
p. cm. -- (Star Wars)
ISBN 978-1-59961-612-4 (v. 1) -- ISBN 978-1-59961-613-1 (v. 2) – ISBN
78-1-59961-614-8 (v. 3) -- ISBN 978-1-59961-615-5 (v. 4)
. Graphic novels. [1. Graphic novels.] I. Lucas, George, 1944- II. Duursema,
an, ill. III. Kryssing, Ray. IV. McCaig, Dave. V. Dutro, Steve. VI. Star wars,
pisode II, attack of the clones (Motion picture) VII. Title.
PZ7.7.G55Epl 2009
[Fic]--dc22

2008038311

Spotlight

All Spotlight books have reinforced library bindings and
are manufactured in the United States of America.

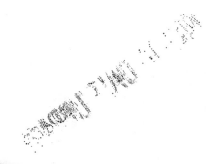

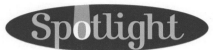

Episode II

ATTACK OF THE CLONES

Volume 1

There is unrest in the Galactic Senate. Several thousand solar systems have declared their intentions to leave the Republic.

This separatist movement, under the leadership of the mysterious Count Dooku, has made it difficult for the limited number of Jedi Knights to maintain peace and order in the galaxy.

Senator Amidala, the former Queen of Naboo, is returning to the Galactic Senate to vote on the critical issue of creating an Army of the Republic to assist the overwhelmed Jedi . . .

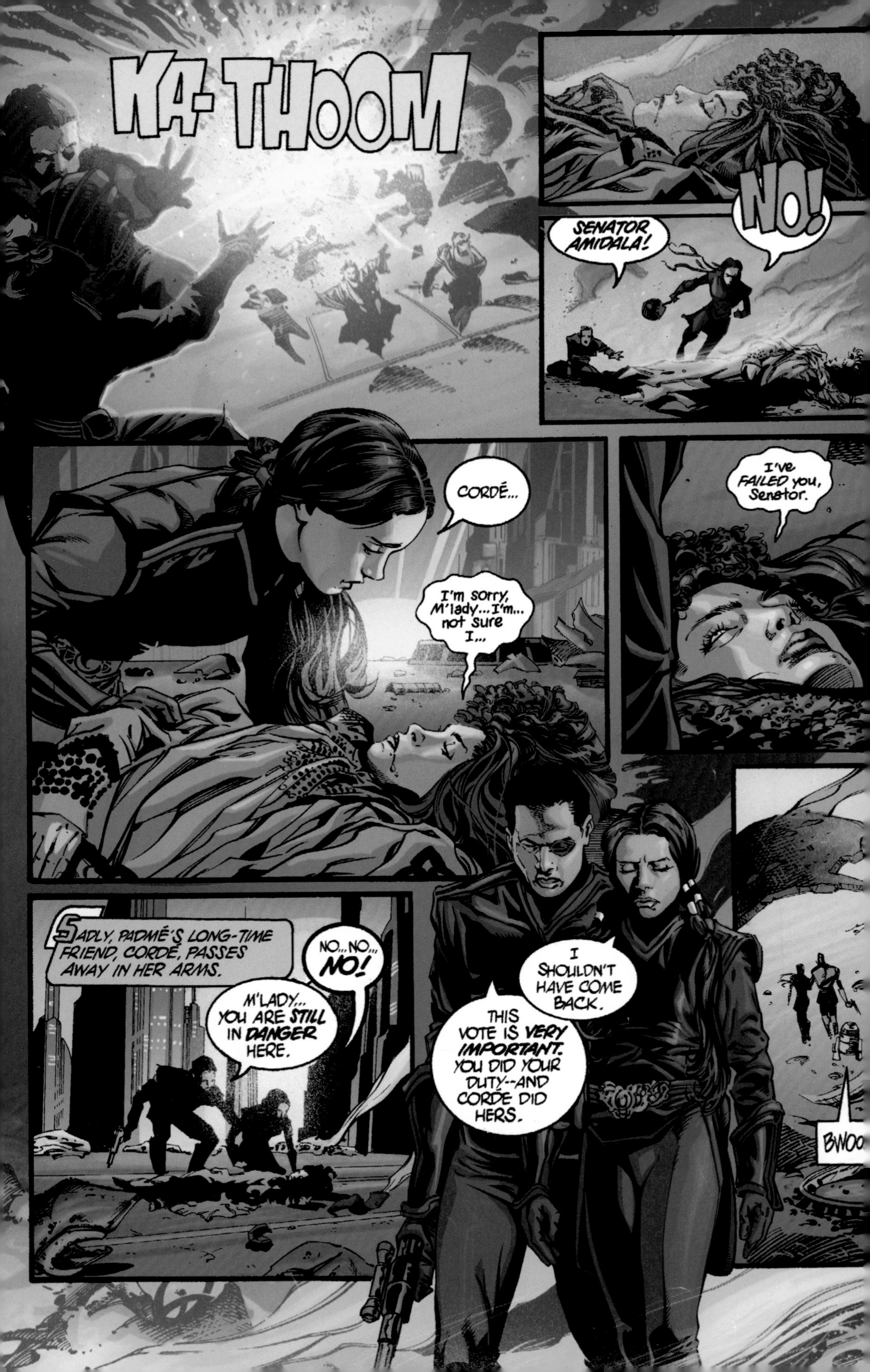
KA-THOOM
SENATOR AMIDALA!
NO!
CORDÉ...
I'm sorry, M'lady... I'm... not sure I...
I've FAILED you, Senator.
SADLY, PADMÉ'S LONG-TIME FRIEND, CORDÉ, PASSES AWAY IN HER ARMS.
NO... NO... NO!
M'LADY... YOU ARE STILL IN DANGER HERE.
I SHOULDN'T HAVE COME BACK.
THIS VOTE IS VERY IMPORTANT. YOU DID YOUR DUTY--AND CORDÉ DID HERS.
BWOO

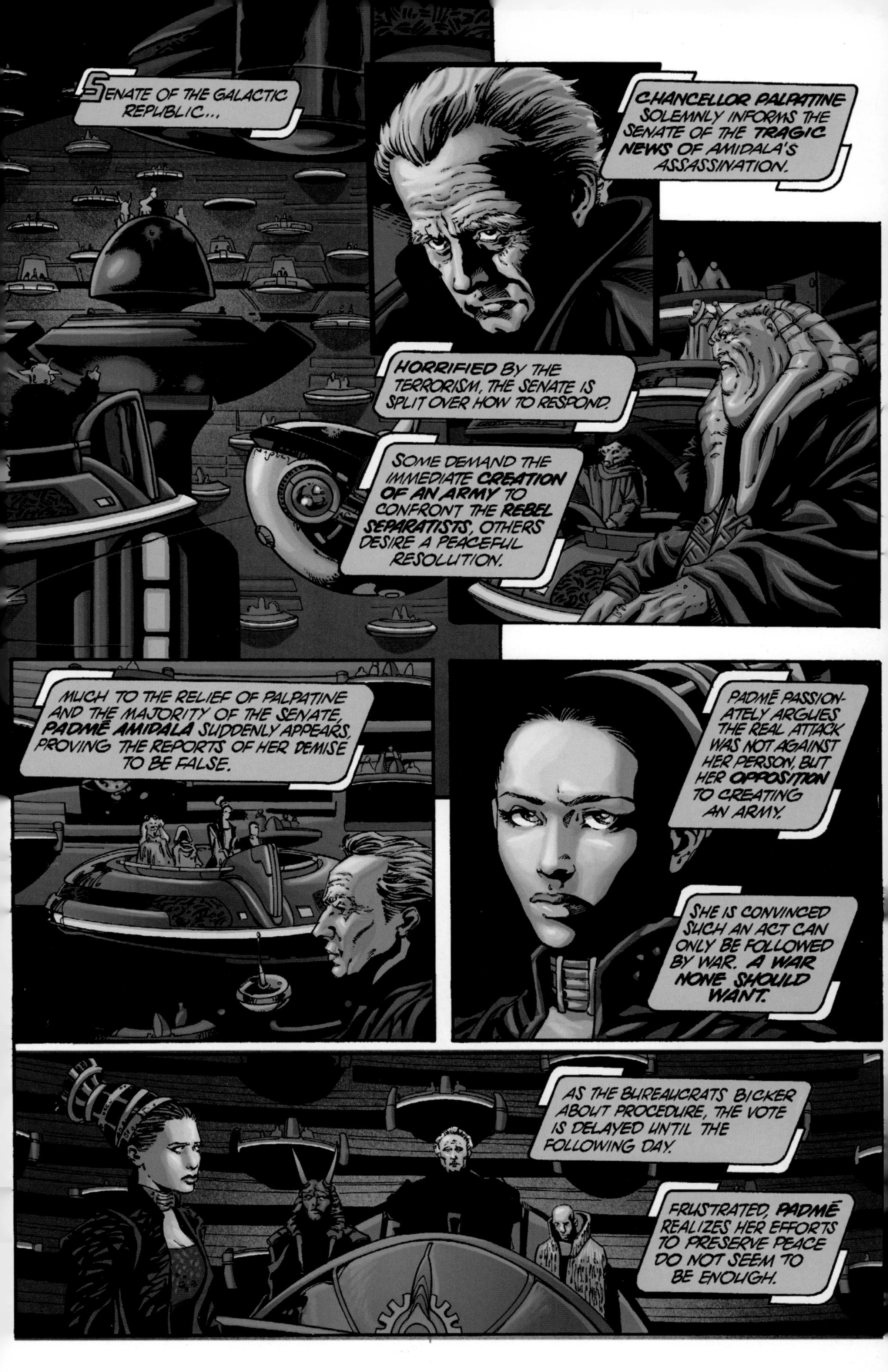
SENATE OF THE GALACTIC REPUBLIC...
CHANCELLOR PALPATINE SOLEMNLY INFORMS THE SENATE OF THE TRAGIC NEWS OF AMIDALA'S ASSASSINATION.
HORRIFIED BY THE TERRORISM, THE SENATE IS SPLIT OVER HOW TO RESPOND.
SOME DEMAND THE IMMEDIATE CREATION OF AN ARMY TO CONFRONT THE REBEL SEPARATISTS, OTHERS DESIRE A PEACEFUL RESOLUTION.
MUCH TO THE RELIEF OF PALPATINE AND THE MAJORITY OF THE SENATE, PADMÉ AMIDALA SUDDENLY APPEARS, PROVING THE REPORTS OF HER DEMISE TO BE FALSE.
PADMÉ PASSION-ATELY ARGUES THE REAL ATTACK WAS NOT AGAINST HER PERSON, BUT HER OPPOSITION TO CREATING AN ARMY.
SHE IS CONVINCED SUCH AN ACT CAN ONLY BE FOLLOWED BY WAR. A WAR NONE SHOULD WANT.
AS THE BUREAUCRATS BICKER ABOUT PROCEDURE, THE VOTE IS DELAYED UNTIL THE FOLLOWING DAY.
FRUSTRATED, PADMÉ REALIZES HER EFFORTS TO PRESERVE PEACE DO NOT SEEM TO BE ENOUGH.

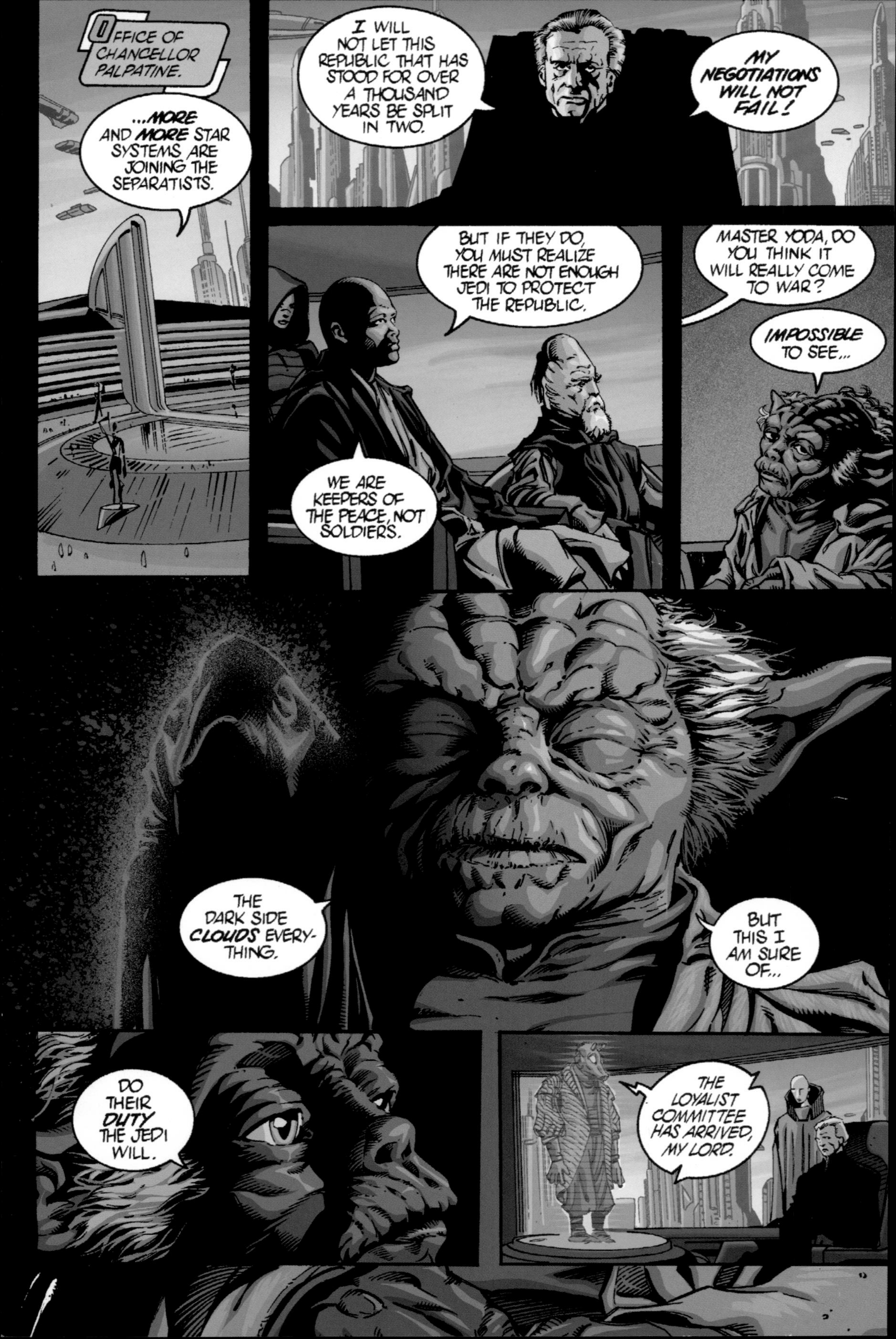
OFFICE OF CHANCELLOR PALPATINE.
...MORE AND MORE STAR SYSTEMS ARE JOINING THE SEPARATISTS.
I WILL NOT LET THIS REPUBLIC THAT HAS STOOD FOR OVER A THOUSAND YEARS BE SPLIT IN TWO.
MY NEGOTIATIONS WILL NOT FAIL!
BUT IF THEY DO, YOU MUST REALIZE THERE ARE NOT ENOUGH JEDI TO PROTECT THE REPUBLIC.
WE ARE KEEPERS OF THE PEACE, NOT SOLDIERS.
MASTER YODA, DO YOU THINK IT WILL REALLY COME TO WAR?
IMPOSSIBLE TO SEE...
THE DARK SIDE CLOUDS EVERY-THING.
BUT THIS I AM SURE OF...
DO THEIR DUTY THE JEDI WILL.
THE LOYALIST COMMITTEE HAS ARRIVED, MY LORD.

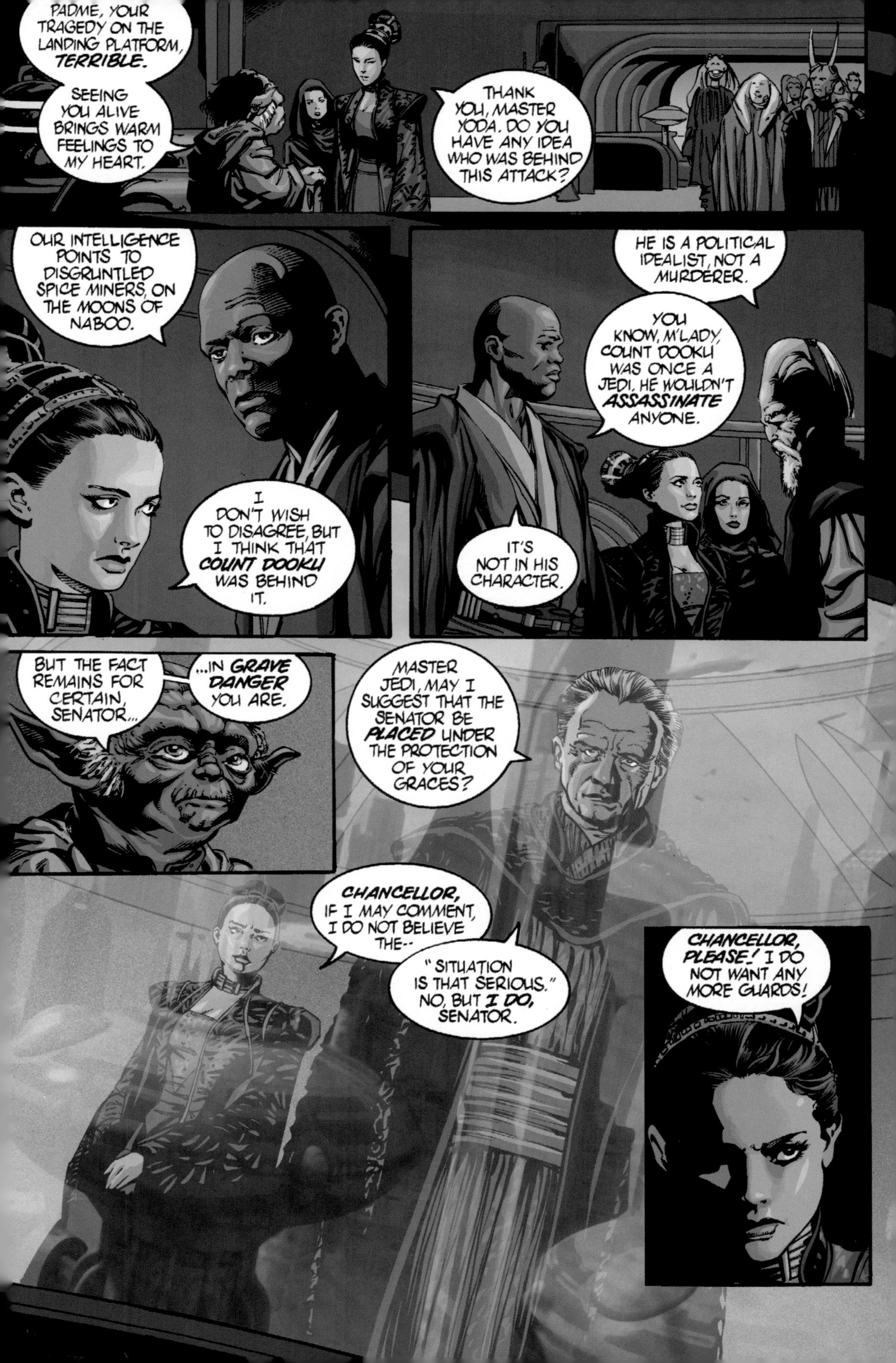
PADME, YOUR TRAGEDY ON THE LANDING PLATFORM, TERRIBLE.
SEEING YOU ALIVE BRINGS WARM FEELINGS TO MY HEART.
THANK YOU, MASTER YODA. DO YOU HAVE ANY IDEA WHO WAS BEHIND THIS ATTACK?
OUR INTELLIGENCE POINTS TO DISGRUNTLED SPICE MINERS, ON THE MOONS OF NABOO.
I DON'T WISH TO DISAGREE, BUT I THINK THAT COUNT DOOKU WAS BEHIND IT.
HE IS A POLITICAL IDEALIST, NOT A MURDERER.
YOU KNOW, M'LADY, COUNT DOOKU WAS ONCE A JEDI. HE WOULDN'T ASSASSINATE ANYONE.
IT'S NOT IN HIS CHARACTER.
BUT THE FACT REMAINS FOR CERTAIN, SENATOR...
...IN GRAVE DANGER YOU ARE.
MASTER JEDI, MAY I SUGGEST THAT THE SENATOR BE PLACED UNDER THE PROTECTION OF YOUR GRACES?
CHANCELLOR, IF I MAY COMMENT, I DO NOT BELIEVE THE--
"SITUATION IS THAT SERIOUS." NO, BUT I DO, SENATOR.
CHANCELLOR, PLEASE! I DO NOT WANT ANY MORE GUARDS!

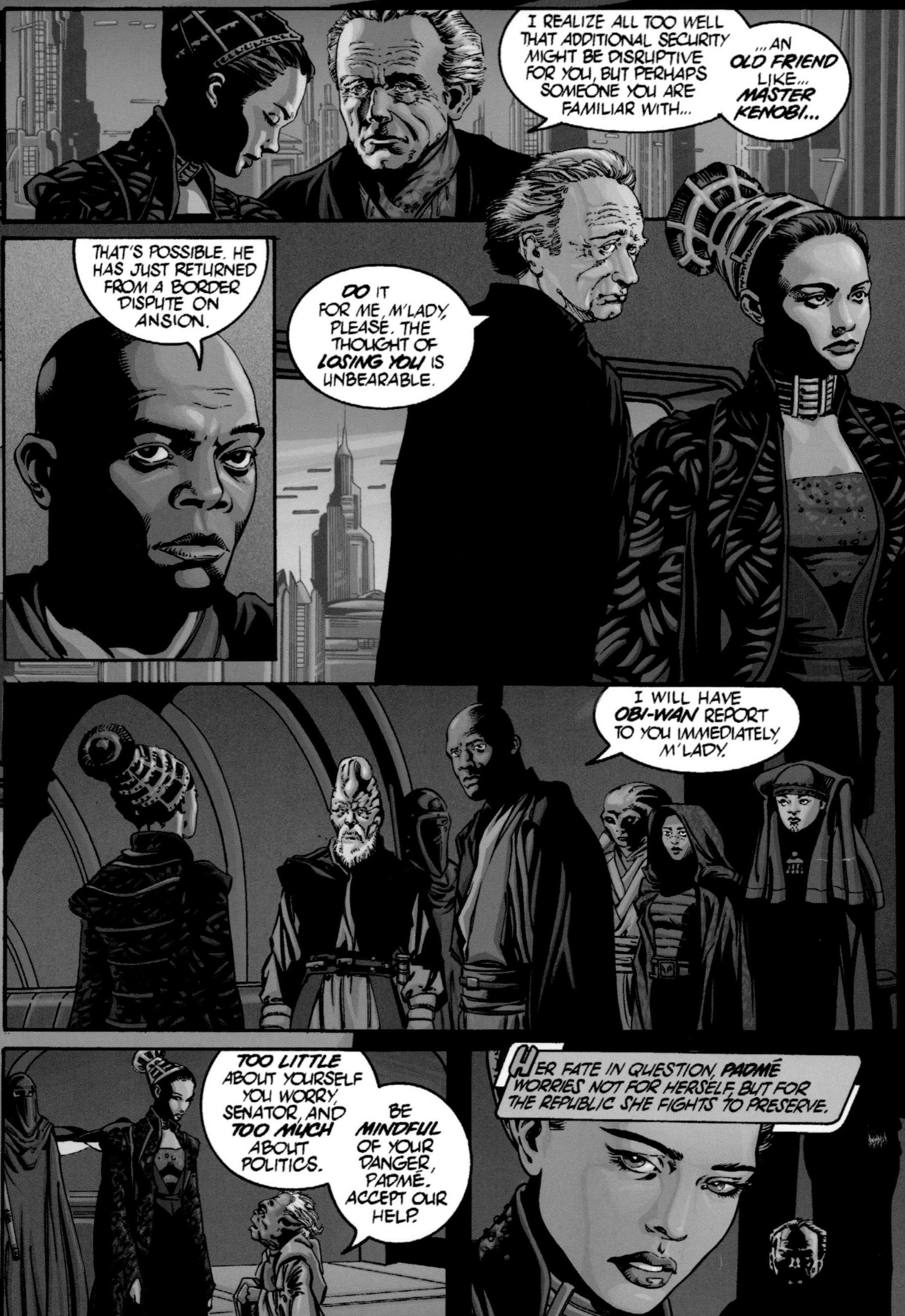
I REALIZE ALL TOO WELL THAT ADDITIONAL SECURITY MIGHT BE DISRUPTIVE FOR YOU, BUT PERHAPS SOMEONE YOU ARE FAMILIAR WITH...
...AN OLD FRIEND LIKE... MASTER KENOBI...
THAT'S POSSIBLE. HE HAS JUST RETURNED FROM A BORDER DISPUTE ON ANSION.
DO IT FOR ME, M'LADY, PLEASE. THE THOUGHT OF LOSING YOU IS UNBEARABLE.
I WILL HAVE OBI-WAN REPORT TO YOU IMMEDIATELY, M'LADY.
TOO LITTLE ABOUT YOURSELF YOU WORRY, SENATOR, AND TOO MUCH ABOUT POLITICS.
BE MINDFUL OF YOUR DANGER, PADMÉ. ACCEPT OUR HELP.
HER FATE IN QUESTION, PADMÉ WORRIES NOT FOR HERSELF, BUT FOR THE REPUBLIC SHE FIGHTS TO PRESERVE.

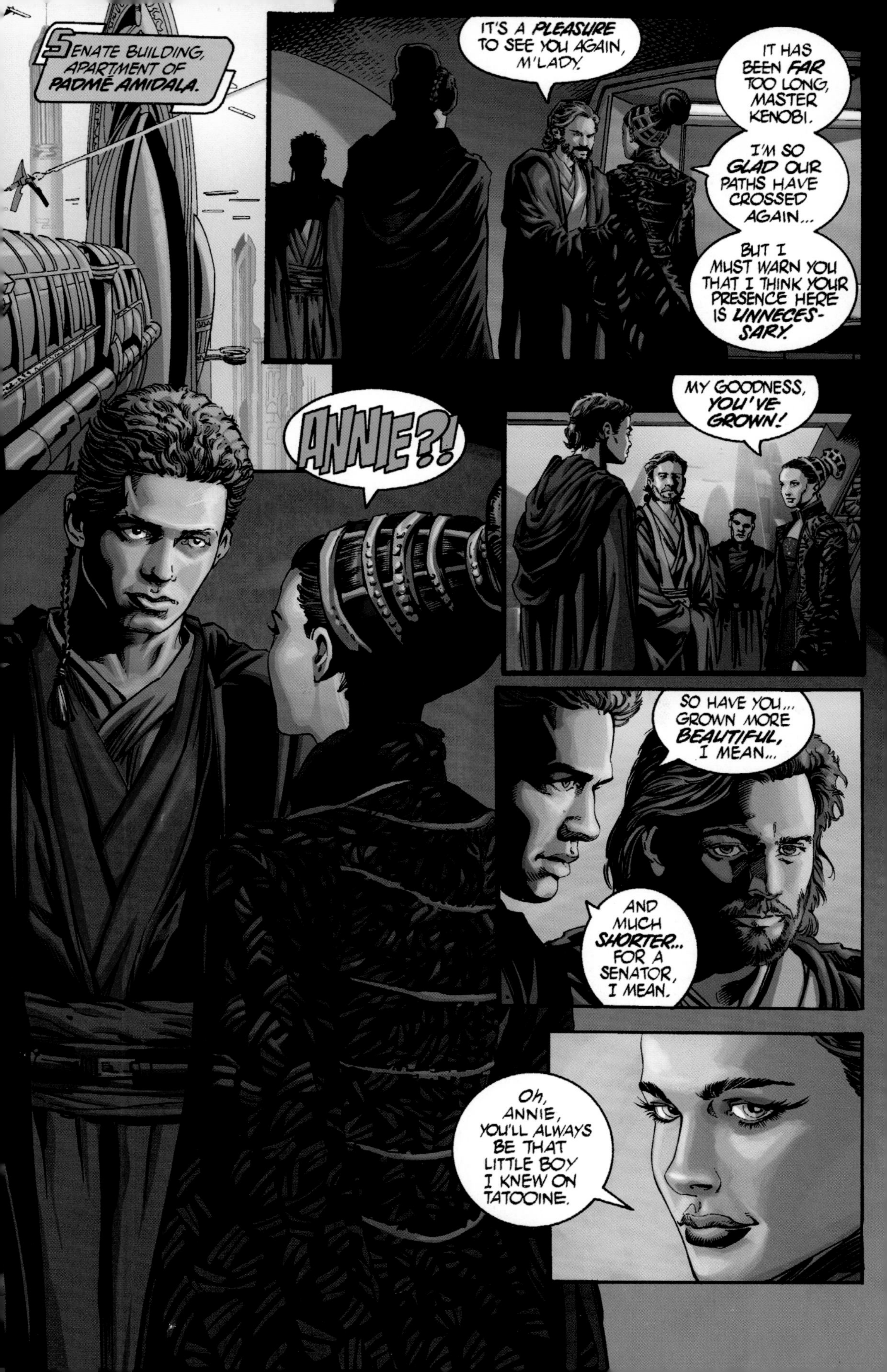
SENATE BUILDING, APARTMENT OF PADMÉ AMIDALA.
IT'S A PLEASURE TO SEE YOU AGAIN, M'LADY.
IT HAS BEEN FAR TOO LONG, MASTER KENOBI.
I'M SO GLAD OUR PATHS HAVE CROSSED AGAIN...
BUT I MUST WARN YOU THAT I THINK YOUR PRESENCE HERE IS UNNECES-SARY.
ANNIE?!
MY GOODNESS, YOU'VE GROWN!
SO HAVE YOU... GROWN MORE BEAUTIFUL, I MEAN...
AND MUCH SHORTER... FOR A SENATOR, I MEAN.
Oh, ANNIE, YOU'LL ALWAYS BE THAT LITTLE BOY I KNEW ON TATOOINE.

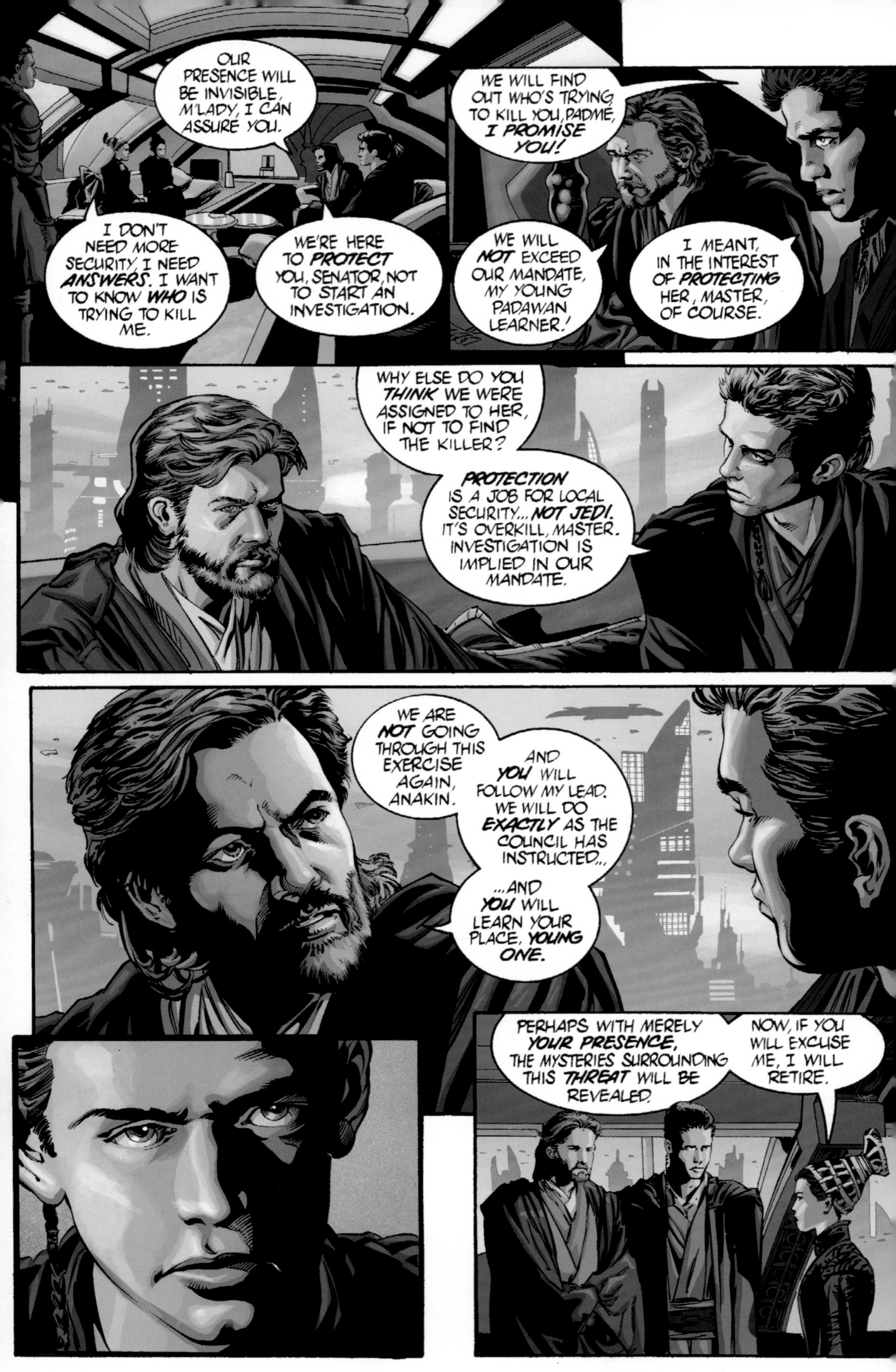
OUR PRESENCE WILL BE INVISIBLE, M'LADY, I CAN ASSURE YOU.
I DON'T NEED MORE SECURITY, I NEED ANSWERS. I WANT TO KNOW WHO IS TRYING TO KILL ME.
WE'RE HERE TO PROTECT YOU, SENATOR, NOT TO START AN INVESTIGATION.
WE WILL FIND OUT WHO'S TRYING TO KILL YOU, PADME, I PROMISE YOU!
WE WILL NOT EXCEED OUR MANDATE, MY YOUNG PADAWAN LEARNER!
I MEANT, IN THE INTEREST OF PROTECTING HER, MASTER, OF COURSE.
WHY ELSE DO YOU THINK WE WERE ASSIGNED TO HER, IF NOT TO FIND THE KILLER?
PROTECTION IS A JOB FOR LOCAL SECURITY... NOT JEDI. IT'S OVERKILL, MASTER. INVESTIGATION IS IMPLIED IN OUR MANDATE.
WE ARE NOT GOING THROUGH THIS EXERCISE AGAIN, ANAKIN.
AND YOU WILL FOLLOW MY LEAD. WE WILL DO EXACTLY AS THE COUNCIL HAS INSTRUCTED...
...AND YOU WILL LEARN YOUR PLACE, YOUNG ONE.
PERHAPS WITH MERELY YOUR PRESENCE, THE MYSTERIES SURROUNDING THIS THREAT WILL BE REVEALED.
NOW, IF YOU WILL EXCUSE ME, I WILL RETIRE.

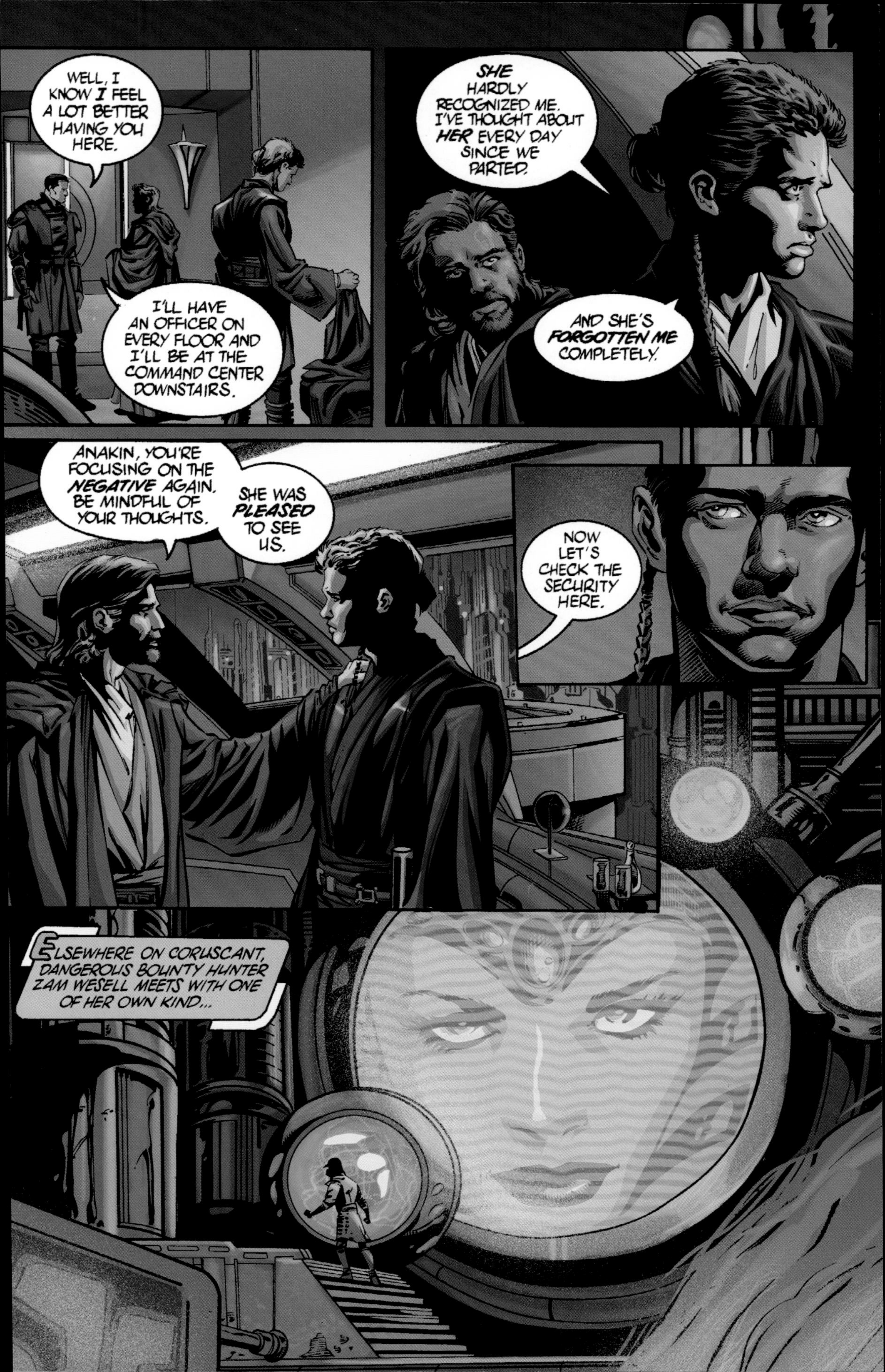
WELL, I KNOW I FEEL A LOT BETTER HAVING YOU HERE.
I'LL HAVE AN OFFICER ON EVERY FLOOR AND I'LL BE AT THE COMMAND CENTER DOWNSTAIRS.
SHE HARDLY RECOGNIZED ME. I'VE THOUGHT ABOUT HER EVERY DAY SINCE WE PARTED.
AND SHE'S FORGOTTEN ME COMPLETELY.
ANAKIN, YOU'RE FOCUSING ON THE NEGATIVE AGAIN. BE MINDFUL OF YOUR THOUGHTS.
SHE WAS PLEASED TO SEE US.
NOW LET'S CHECK THE SECURITY HERE.
ELSEWHERE ON CORUSCANT, DANGEROUS BOUNTY HUNTER ZAM WESELL MEETS WITH ONE OF HER OWN KIND...

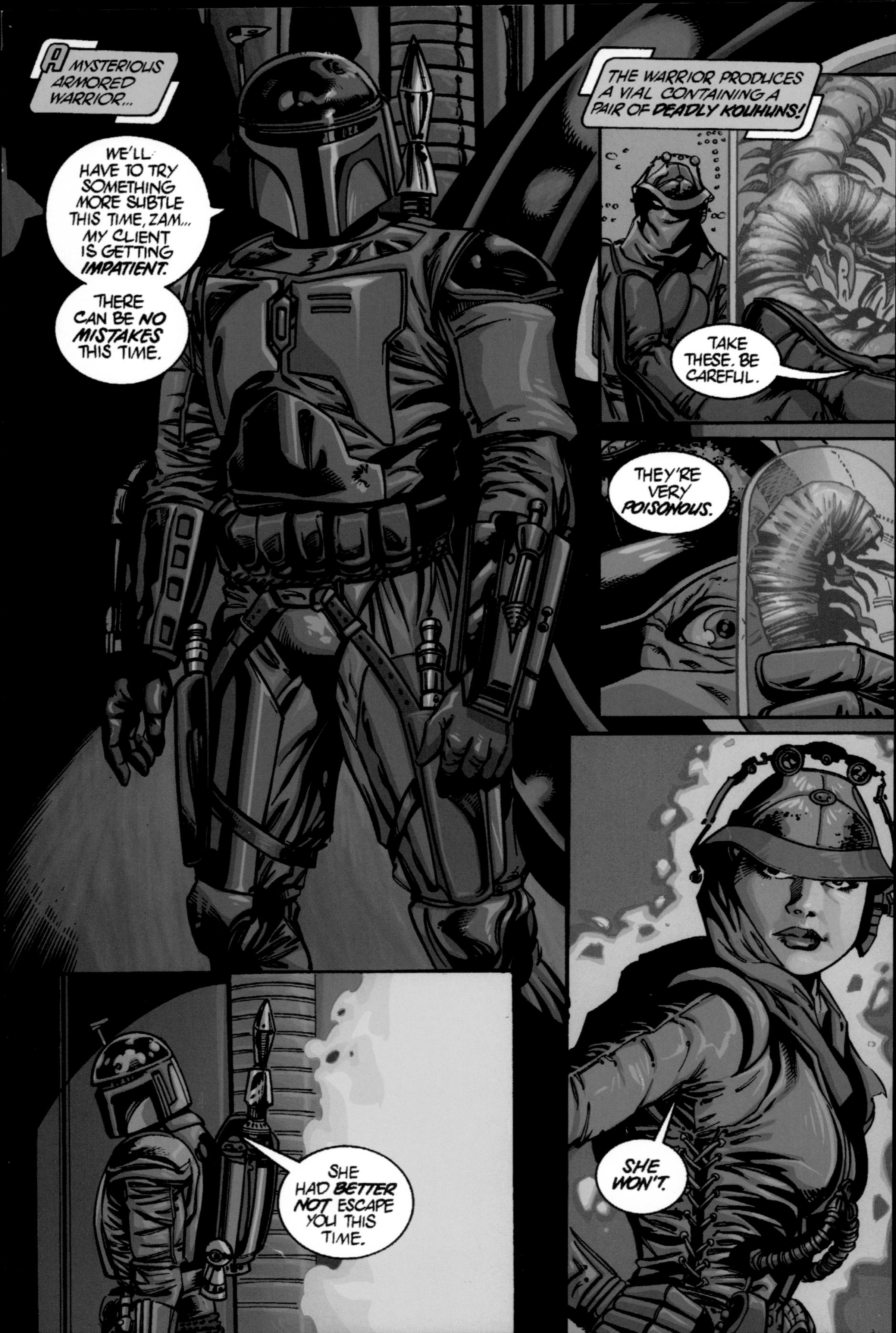
A MYSTERIOUS ARMORED WARRIOR...
WE'LL HAVE TO TRY SOMETHING MORE SUBTLE THIS TIME, ZAM... MY CLIENT IS GETTING IMPATIENT.
THERE CAN BE NO MISTAKES THIS TIME.
THE WARRIOR PRODUCES A VIAL CONTAINING A PAIR OF DEADLY KOUHUNS!
TAKE THESE. BE CAREFUL.
THEY'RE VERY POISONOUS.
SHE HAD BETTER NOT ESCAPE YOU THIS TIME.
SHE WON'T.

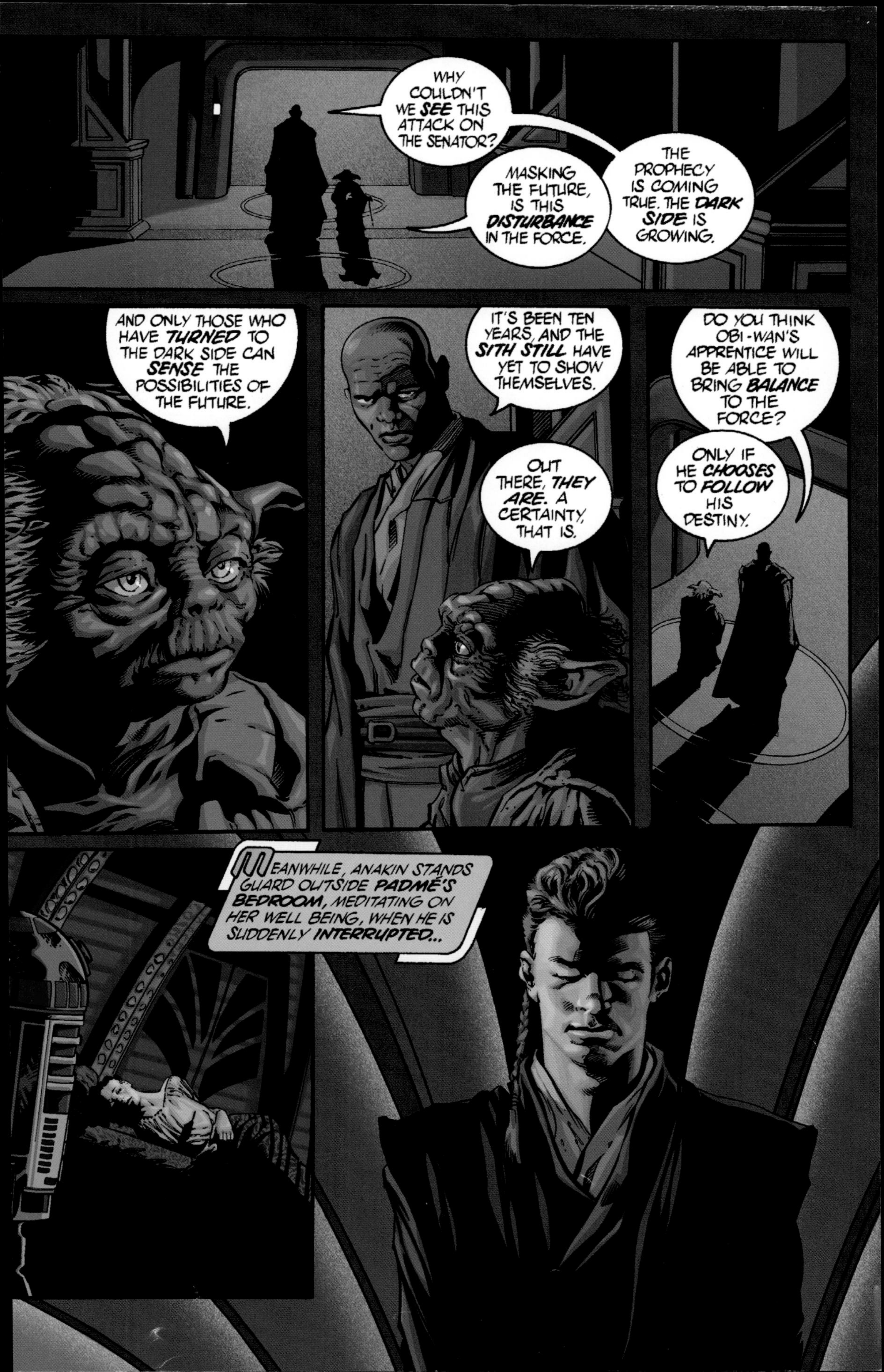
WHY COULDN'T WE SEE THIS ATTACK ON THE SENATOR?
MASKING THE FUTURE, IS THIS DISTURBANCE IN THE FORCE.
THE PROPHECY IS COMING TRUE. THE DARK SIDE IS GROWING.
AND ONLY THOSE WHO HAVE TURNED TO THE DARK SIDE CAN SENSE THE POSSIBILITIES OF THE FUTURE.
IT'S BEEN TEN YEARS, AND THE SITH STILL HAVE YET TO SHOW THEMSELVES.
OUT THERE, THEY ARE. A CERTAINTY, THAT IS.
DO YOU THINK OBI-WAN'S APPRENTICE WILL BE ABLE TO BRING BALANCE TO THE FORCE?
ONLY IF HE CHOOSES TO FOLLOW HIS DESTINY.
MEANWHILE, ANAKIN STANDS GUARD OUTSIDE PADMÉ'S BEDROOM, MEDITATING ON HER WELL BEING, WHEN HE IS SUDDENLY INTERRUPTED...

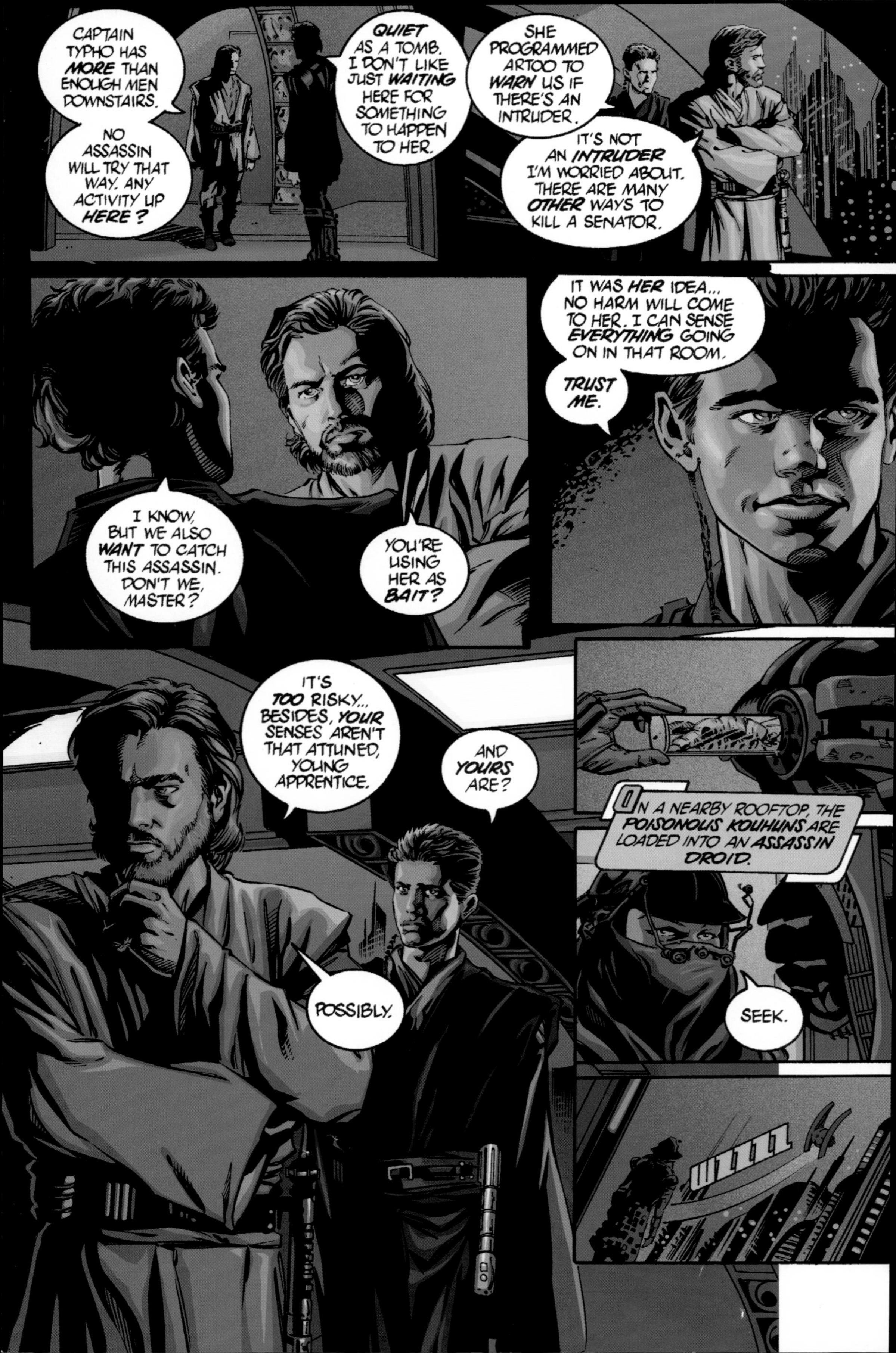
CAPTAIN TYPHO HAS MORE THAN ENOUGH MEN DOWNSTAIRS.
NO ASSASSIN WILL TRY THAT WAY. ANY ACTIVITY UP HERE?
QUIET AS A TOMB. I DON'T LIKE JUST WAITING HERE FOR SOMETHING TO HAPPEN TO HER.
SHE PROGRAMMED ARTOO TO WARN US IF THERE'S AN INTRUDER.
IT'S NOT AN INTRUDER I'M WORRIED ABOUT. THERE ARE MANY OTHER WAYS TO KILL A SENATOR.
I KNOW, BUT WE ALSO WANT TO CATCH THIS ASSASSIN. DON'T WE, MASTER?
YOU'RE USING HER AS BAIT?
IT WAS HER IDEA... NO HARM WILL COME TO HER. I CAN SENSE EVERYTHING GOING ON IN THAT ROOM.
TRUST ME.
IT'S TOO RISKY... BESIDES, YOUR SENSES AREN'T THAT ATTUNED, YOUNG APPRENTICE.
AND YOURS ARE?
POSSIBLY.
ON A NEARBY ROOFTOP, THE POISONOUS KOUHUNS ARE LOADED INTO AN ASSASSIN DROID.
SEEK.
WZZZZ

UNAWARE OF THE APPROACHING DANGER, *ANAKIN* AND *OBI-WAN* CONVERSE...

I DON'T SLEEP WELL ANYMORE.

BECAUSE OF YOUR *MOTHER*?

I DON'T KNOW WHY I KEEP *DREAMING* ABOUT HER NOW. I HAVEN'T SEEN *HER* SINCE I WAS LITTLE.

DREAMS PASS IN TIME.

I'D RATHER DREAM OF *PADMÉ.* JUST BEING AROUND HER AGAIN IS...

INTOXI-CATING.

MIND YOUR THOUGHTS, ANAKIN, THEY *BETRAY* YOU.

YOU! I'VE MADE A COMMITMENT TO THE JEDI ORDER... A *COMMITMENT* NOT EASILY BROKEN.

AND DON'T FORGET SHE'S A POLITICIAN. THEY'RE *NOT* TO BE TRUSTED.

AND THEY *FORGET THE NICETIES* OF DEMOCRACY TO GET THOSE FUNDS.

IT'S BEEN MY EXPERIENCE THAT SENATORS ARE ONLY FOCUSED ON *PLEASING THOSE* WHO FUND THEIR CAMPAIGNS.

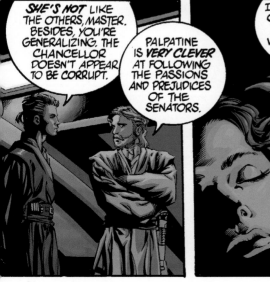

SHE'S NOT LIKE THE OTHERS, MASTER. BESIDES, YOU'RE GENERALIZING. THE CHANCELLOR DOESN'T APPEAR TO BE CORRUPT.

PALPATINE IS *VERY CLEVER* AT FOLLOWING THE PASSIONS AND PREJUDICES OF THE SENATORS.

I *THINK* HE IS A GOOD MAN. MY INSTINCTS ARE VERY *POSITIVE* ABOUT HIM.

MASTER...

I SENSE IT, TOO!

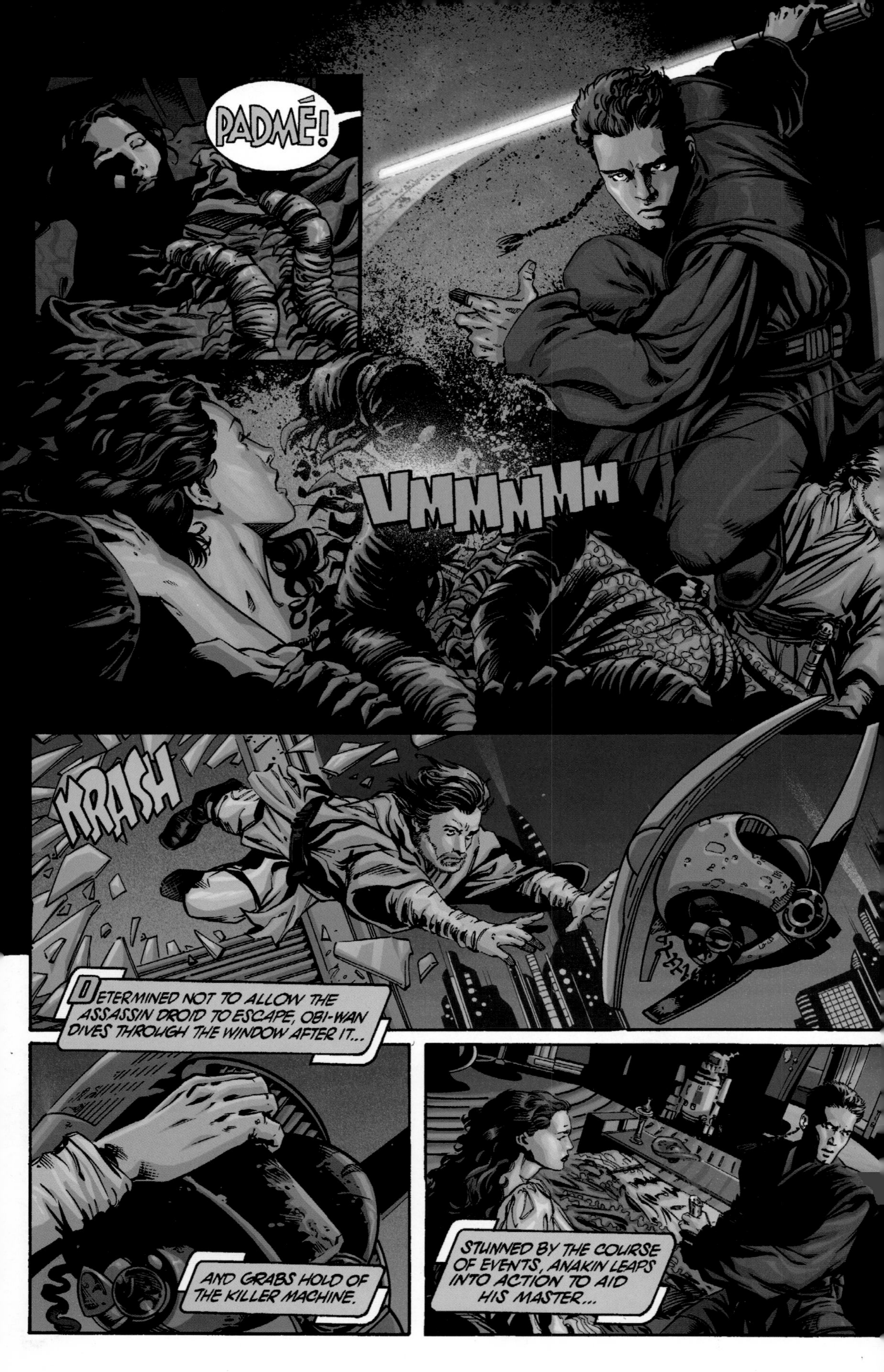
PADMÉ!
UMMMMMM
KRASH
DETERMINED NOT TO ALLOW THE ASSASSIN DROID TO ESCAPE, OBI-WAN DIVES THROUGH THE WINDOW AFTER IT...
AND GRABS HOLD OF THE KILLER MACHINE.
STUNNED BY THE COURSE OF EVENTS, ANAKIN LEAPS INTO ACTION TO AID HIS MASTER...

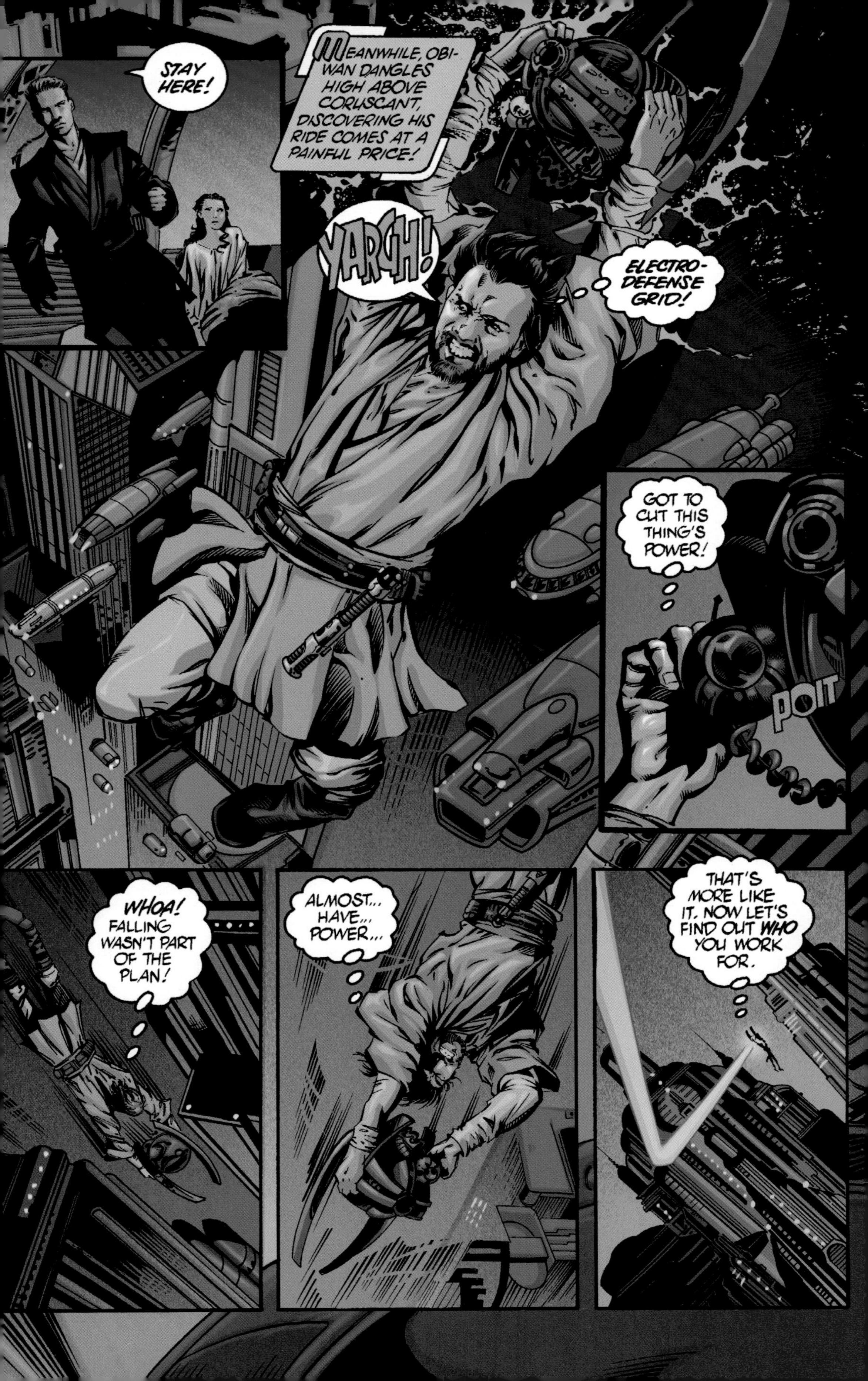
STAY HERE!
MEANWHILE, OBI-WAN DANGLES HIGH ABOVE CORUSCANT, DISCOVERING HIS RIDE COMES AT A PAINFUL PRICE!
YARGH!
ELECTRO-DEFENSE GRID!
GOT TO CUT THIS THING'S POWER!
POIT
WHOA! FALLING WASN'T PART OF THE PLAN!
ALMOST... HAVE... POWER...
THAT'S MORE LIKE IT. NOW LET'S FIND OUT WHO YOU WORK FOR.

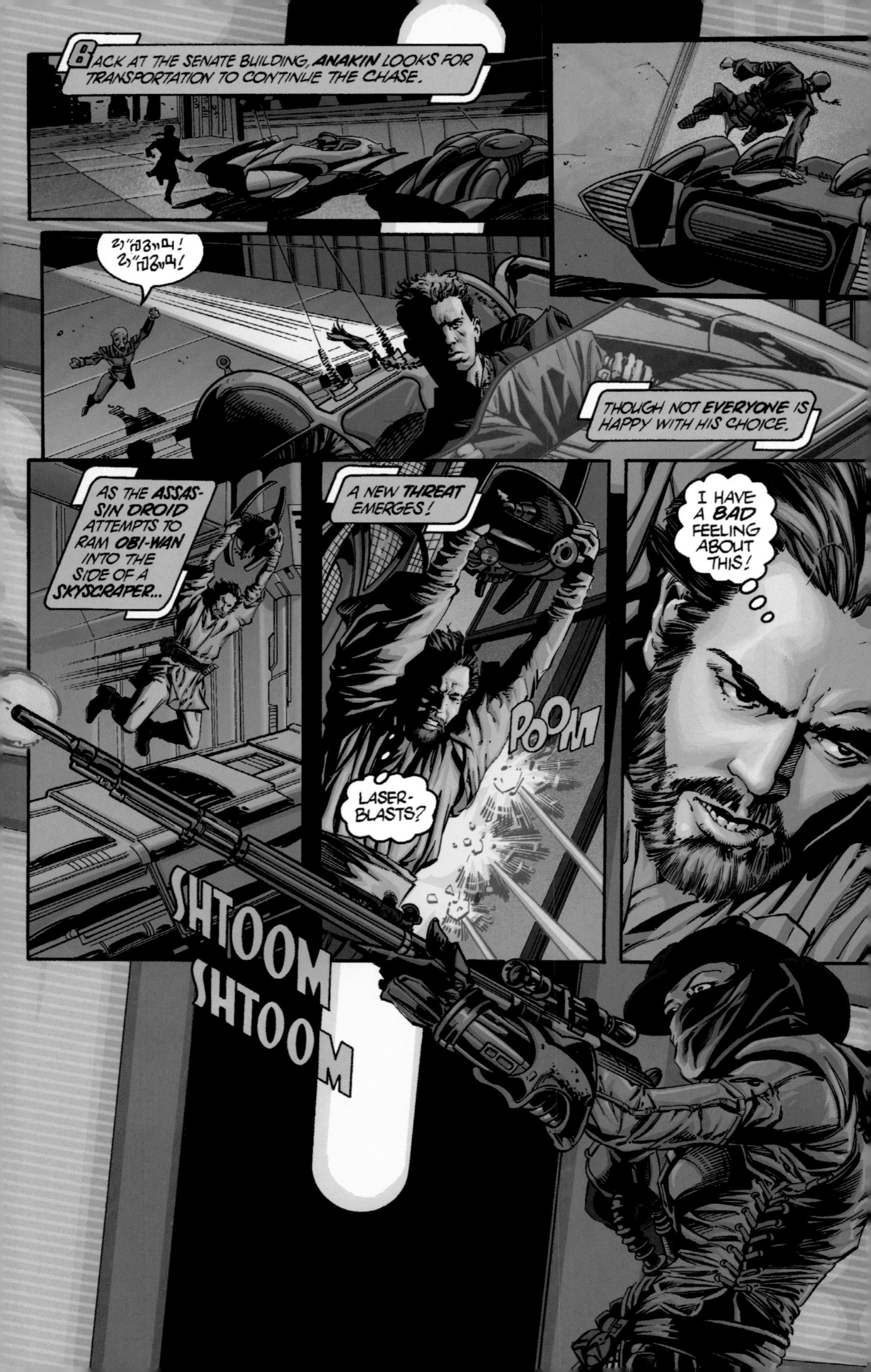
BACK AT THE SENATE BUILDING, ANAKIN LOOKS FOR TRANSPORTATION TO CONTINUE THE CHASE.
THOUGH NOT EVERYONE IS HAPPY WITH HIS CHOICE.
AS THE ASSAS-SIN DROID ATTEMPTS TO RAM OBI-WAN INTO THE SIDE OF A SKYSCRAPER...
A NEW THREAT EMERGES!
POOM
LASER-BLASTS?
I HAVE A BAD FEELING ABOUT THIS!
SHTOOM
SHTOOM

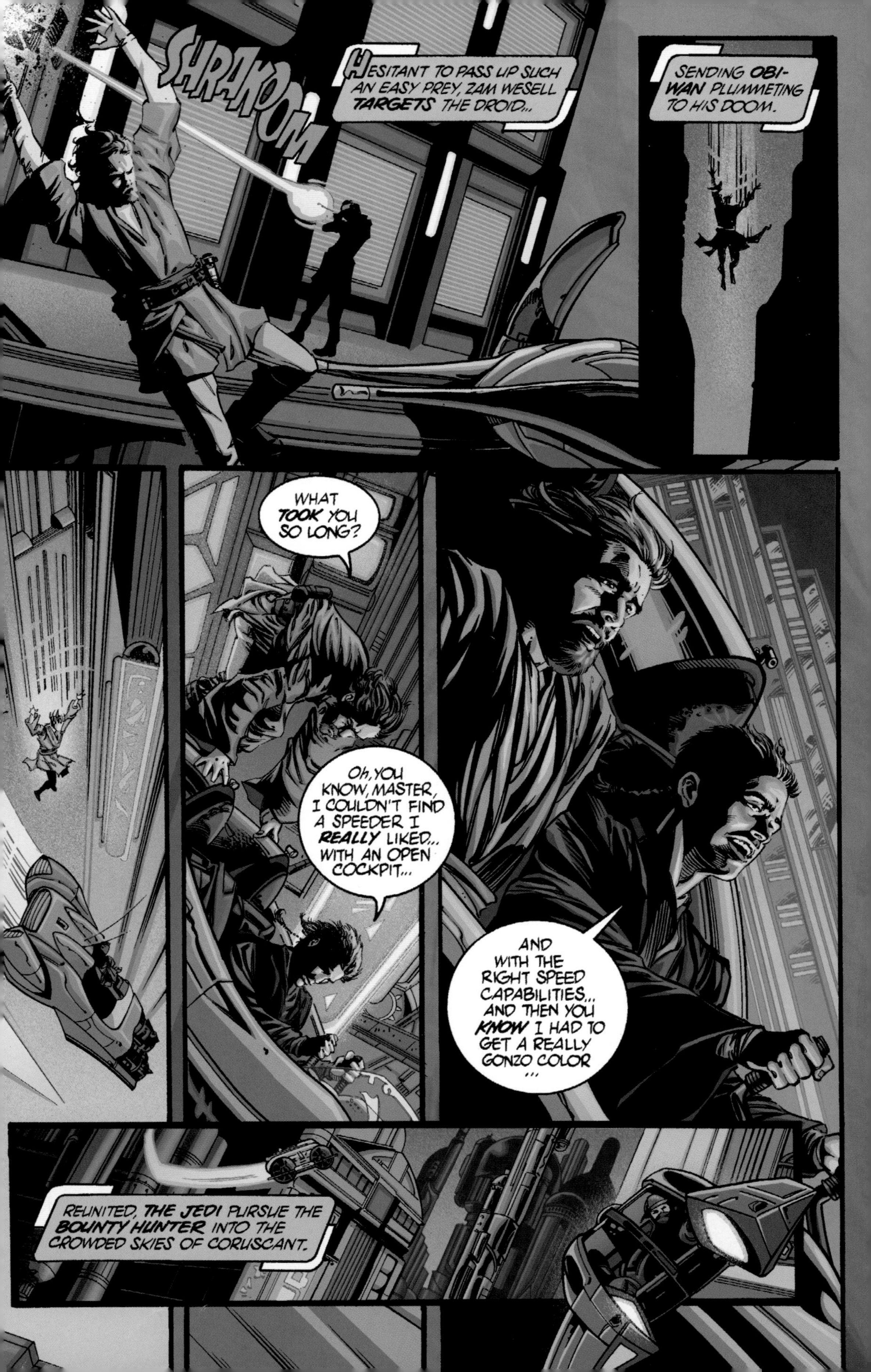
SHRAKOOM
HESITANT TO PASS UP SUCH AN EASY PREY, ZAM WESELL TARGETS THE DROID...
SENDING OBI-WAN PLUMMETING TO HIS DOOM.
WHAT TOOK YOU SO LONG?
Oh, YOU KNOW, MASTER, I COULDN'T FIND A SPEEDER I REALLY LIKED... WITH AN OPEN COCKPIT...
AND WITH THE RIGHT SPEED CAPABILITIES... AND THEN YOU KNOW I HAD TO GET A REALLY GONZO COLOR ...
REUNITED, THE JEDI PURSUE THE BOUNTY HUNTER INTO THE CROWDED SKIES OF CORUSCANT.

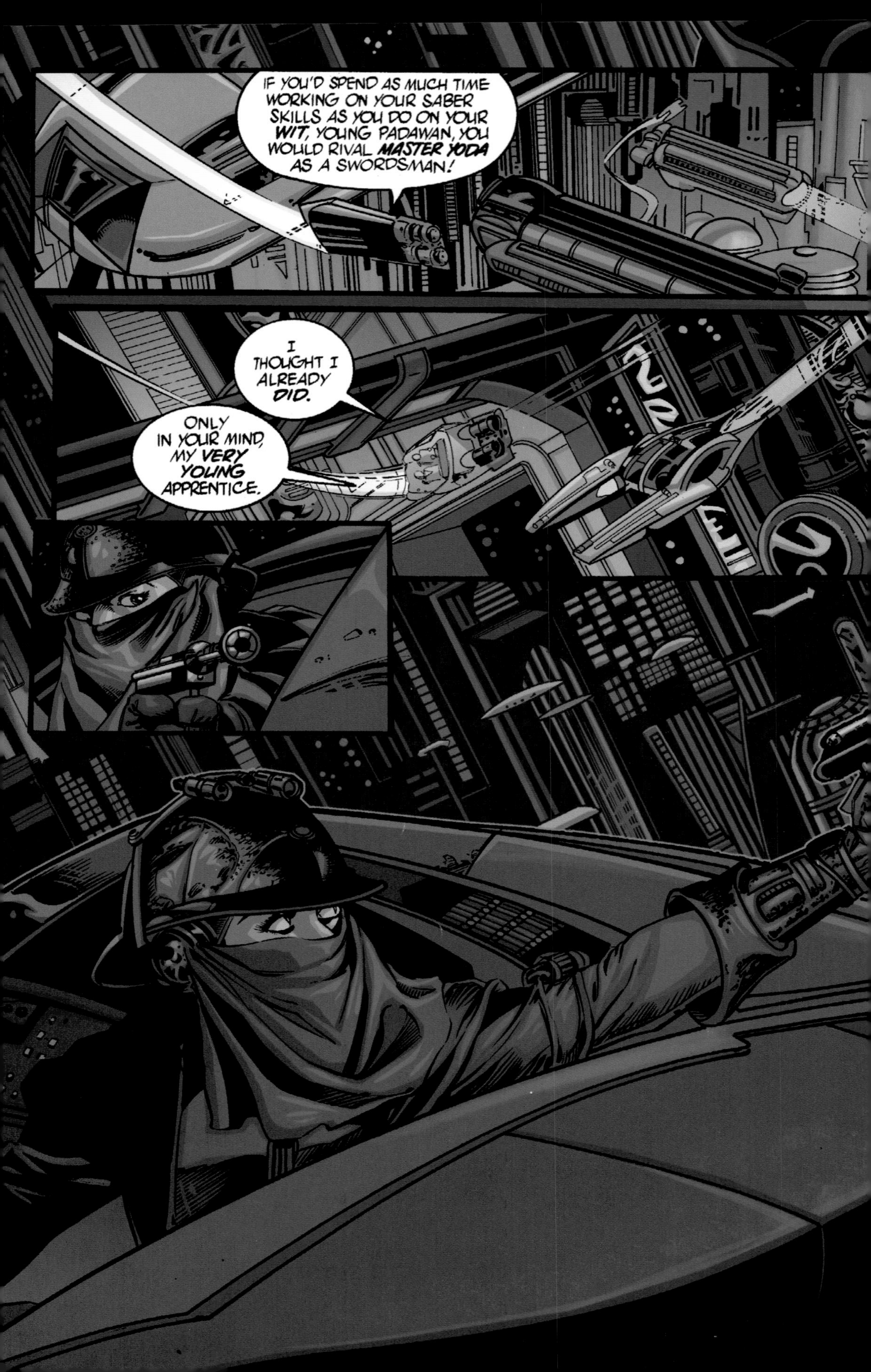
IF YOU'D SPEND AS MUCH TIME WORKING ON YOUR SABER SKILLS AS YOU DO ON YOUR **WIT**, YOUNG PADAWAN, YOU WOULD RIVAL **MASTER YODA** AS A SWORDSMAN!
I THOUGHT I ALREADY **DID.**
ONLY IN YOUR MIND, MY **VERY YOUNG** APPRENTICE.

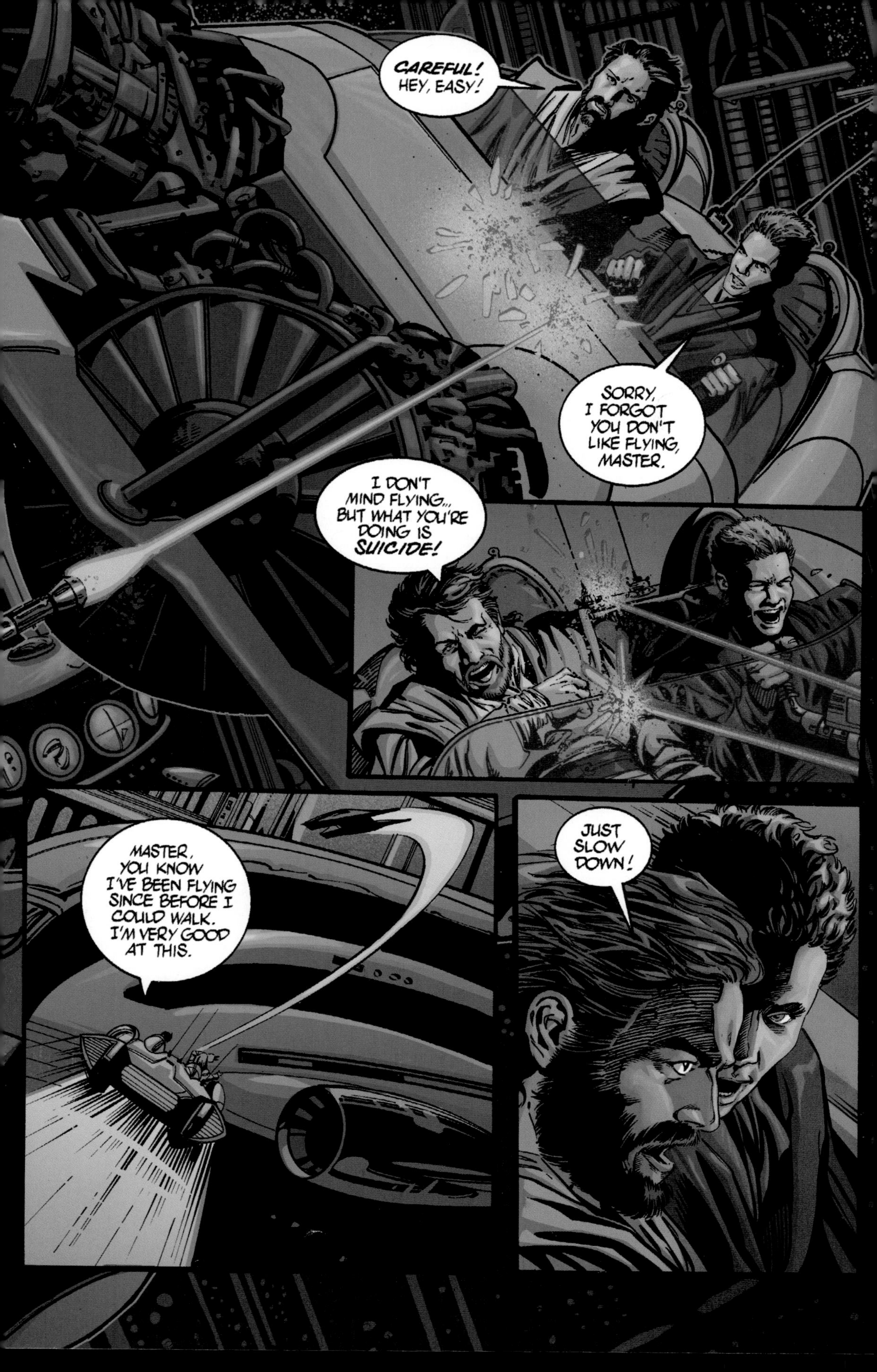
CAREFUL! HEY, EASY!
SORRY, I FORGOT YOU DON'T LIKE FLYING, MASTER.
I DON'T MIND FLYING... BUT WHAT YOU'RE DOING IS SUICIDE!
MASTER, YOU KNOW I'VE BEEN FLYING SINCE BEFORE I COULD WALK. I'M VERY GOOD AT THIS.
JUST SLOW DOWN!

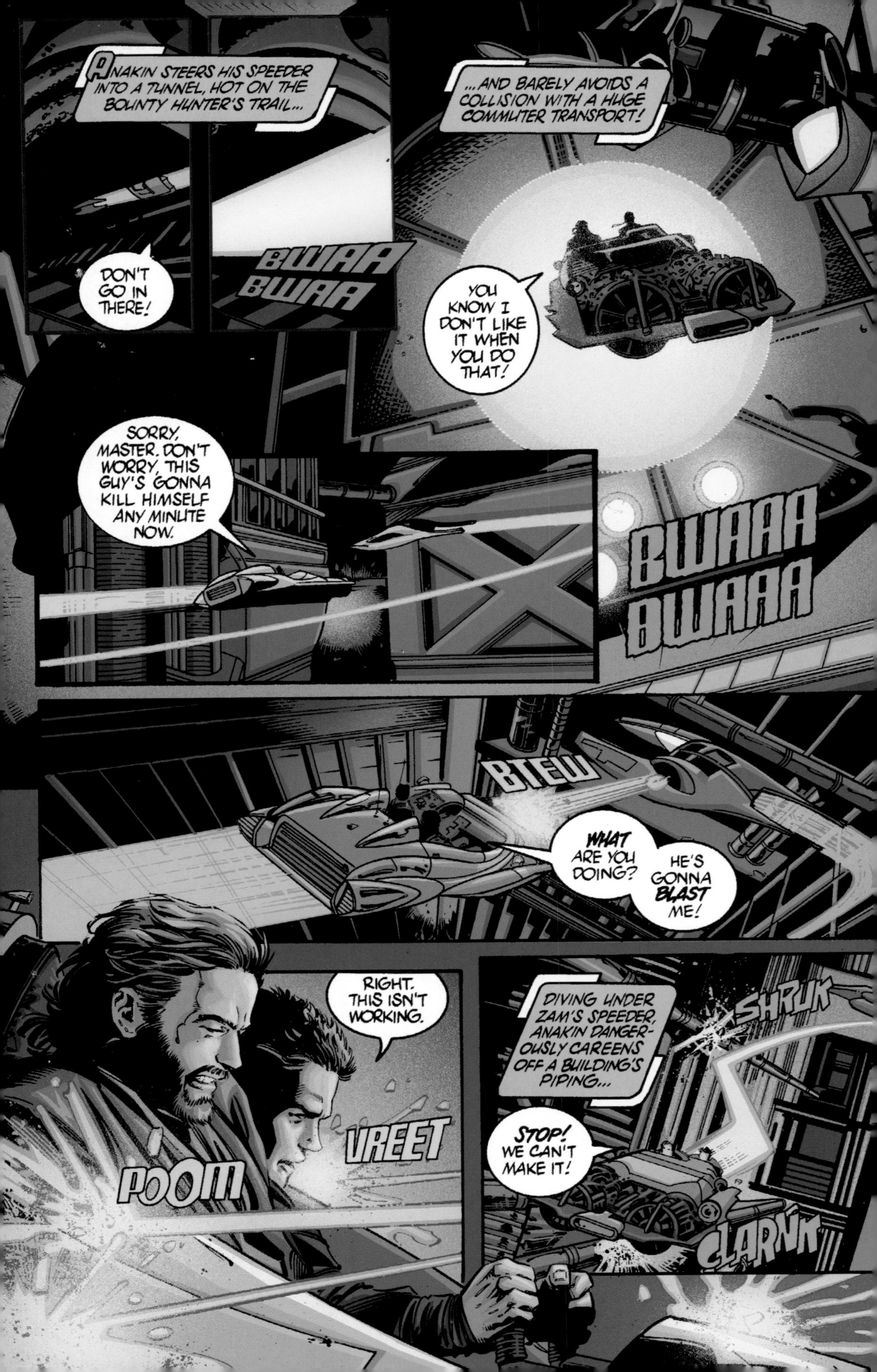
ANAKIN STEERS HIS SPEEDER INTO A TUNNEL, HOT ON THE BOUNTY HUNTER'S TRAIL...
DON'T GO IN THERE!
BWAA BWAA
...AND BARELY AVOIDS A COLLISION WITH A HUGE COMMUTER TRANSPORT!
YOU KNOW I DON'T LIKE IT WHEN YOU DO THAT!
SORRY, MASTER. DON'T WORRY, THIS GUY'S GONNA KILL HIMSELF ANY MINUTE NOW.
BWAAA BWAAA
BTEW
WHAT ARE YOU DOING?
HE'S GONNA BLAST ME!
RIGHT. THIS ISN'T WORKING.
VREET
POOM
DIVING UNDER ZAM'S SPEEDER, ANAKIN DANGEROUSLY CAREENS OFF A BUILDING'S PIPING...
SHRUK
STOP! WE CAN'T MAKE IT!
CLARNK

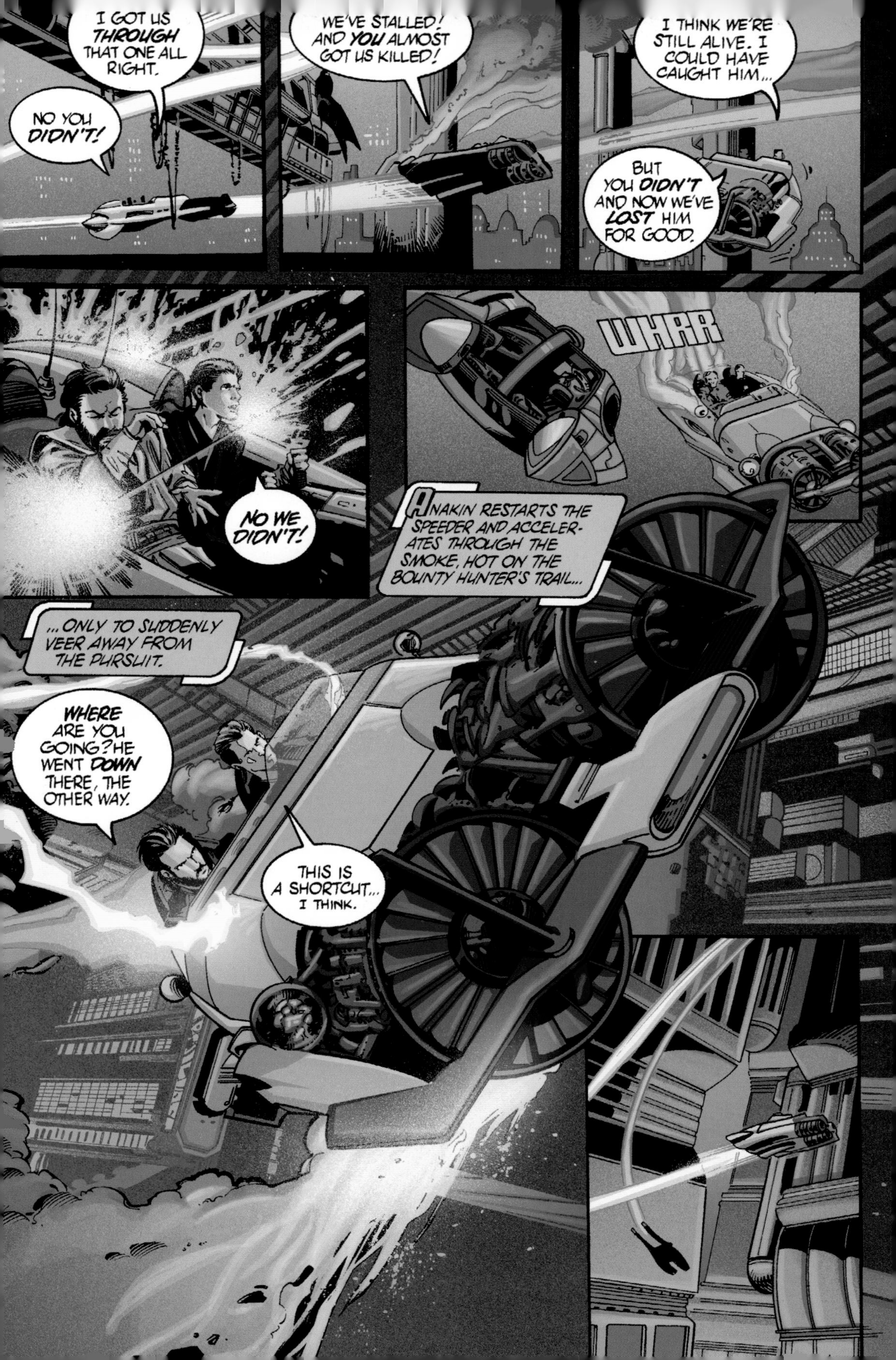

I GOT US THROUGH THAT ONE ALL RIGHT.
NO YOU DIDN'T!
WE'VE STALLED! AND YOU ALMOST GOT US KILLED!
I THINK WE'RE STILL ALIVE. I COULD HAVE CAUGHT HIM...
BUT YOU DIDN'T AND NOW WE'VE LOST HIM FOR GOOD.
NO WE DIDN'T!
WHRR
ANAKIN RESTARTS THE SPEEDER AND ACCELERATES THROUGH THE SMOKE, HOT ON THE BOUNTY HUNTER'S TRAIL...
...ONLY TO SUDDENLY VEER AWAY FROM THE PURSUIT.
WHERE ARE YOU GOING? HE WENT DOWN THERE, THE OTHER WAY.
THIS IS A SHORTCUT... I THINK.

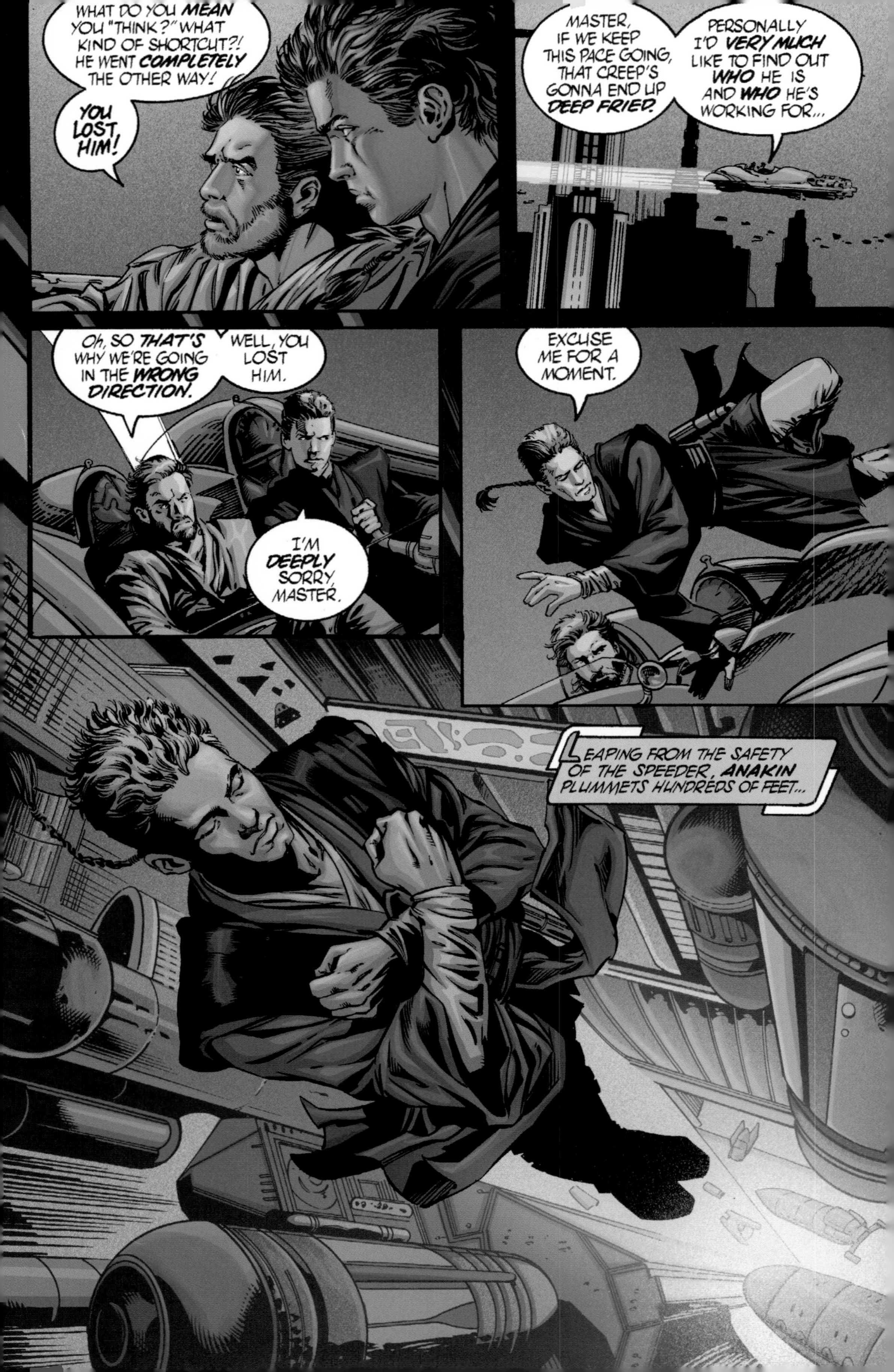
WHAT DO YOU MEAN YOU "THINK?" WHAT KIND OF SHORTCUT?! HE WENT COMPLETELY THE OTHER WAY!
YOU LOST HIM!
MASTER, IF WE KEEP THIS PACE GOING, THAT CREEP'S GONNA END UP DEEP FRIED.
PERSONALLY I'D VERY MUCH LIKE TO FIND OUT WHO HE IS AND WHO HE'S WORKING FOR...
Oh, SO THAT'S WHY WE'RE GOING IN THE WRONG DIRECTION.
WELL, YOU LOST HIM.
I'M DEEPLY SORRY, MASTER.
EXCUSE ME FOR A MOMENT.
LEAPING FROM THE SAFETY OF THE SPEEDER, ANAKIN PLUMMETS HUNDREDS OF FEET...

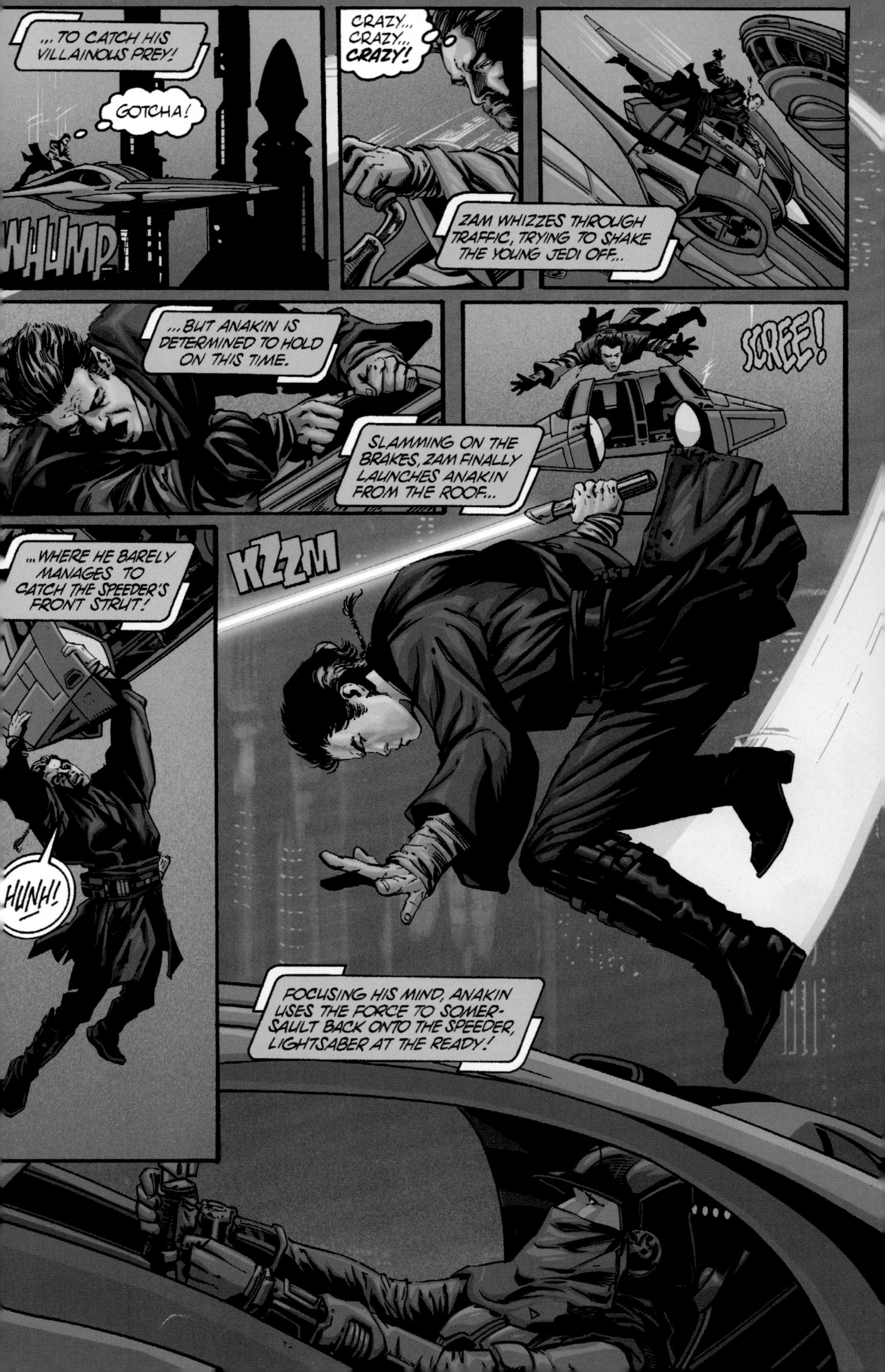
...TO CATCH HIS VILLAINOUS PREY!
GOTCHA!
WHUMP
CRAZY... CRAZY... CRAZY!
ZAM WHIZZES THROUGH TRAFFIC, TRYING TO SHAKE THE YOUNG JEDI OFF...
...BUT ANAKIN IS DETERMINED TO HOLD ON THIS TIME.
SCREE!
SLAMMING ON THE BRAKES, ZAM FINALLY LAUNCHES ANAKIN FROM THE ROOF...
...WHERE HE BARELY MANAGES TO CATCH THE SPEEDER'S FRONT STRUT!
KZZM
HUNH!
FOCUSING HIS MIND, ANAKIN USES THE FORCE TO SOMER-SAULT BACK ONTO THE SPEEDER, LIGHTSABER AT THE READY!

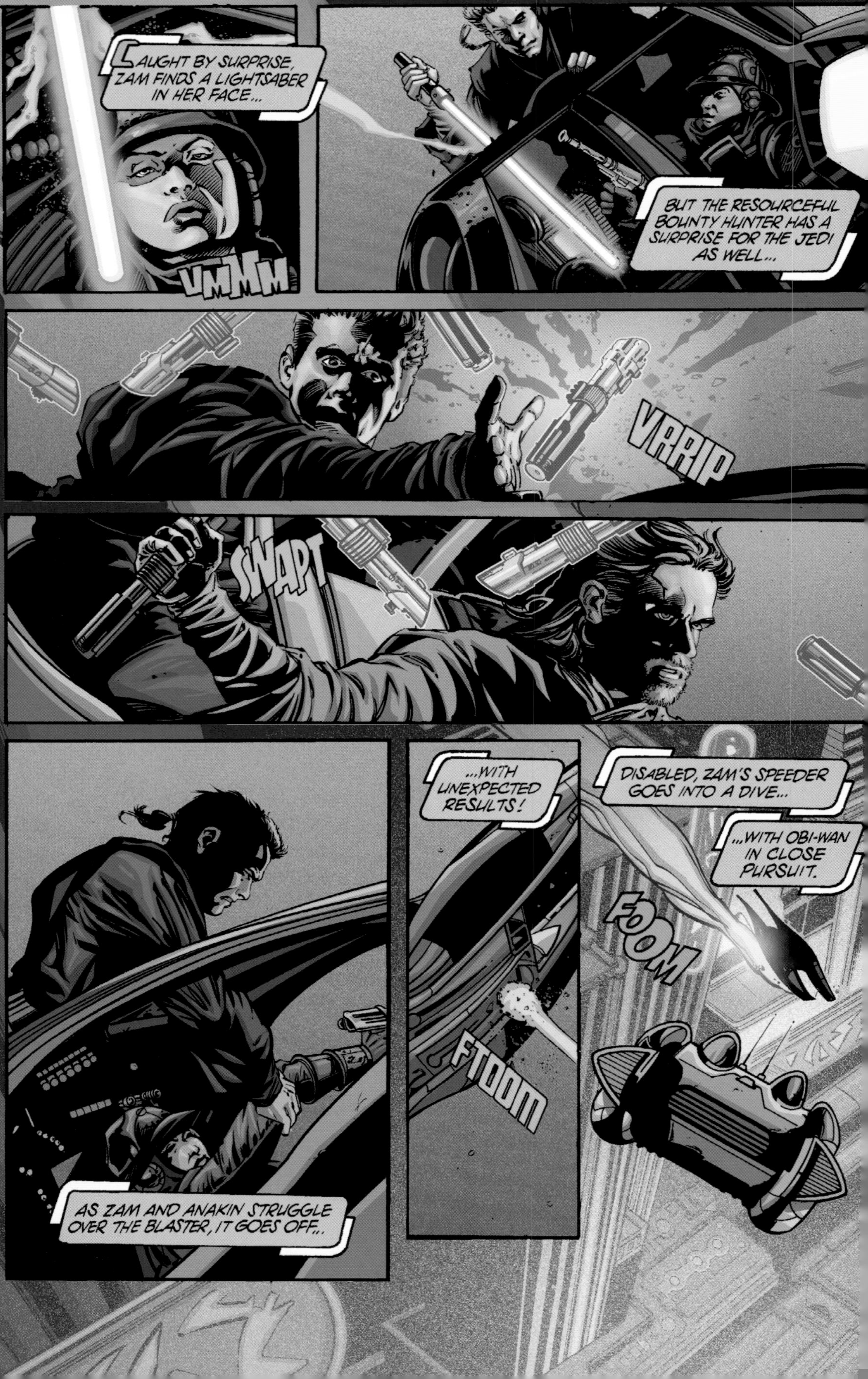
CAUGHT BY SURPRISE, ZAM FINDS A LIGHTSABER IN HER FACE...
UMMM
BUT THE RESOURCEFUL BOUNTY HUNTER HAS A SURPRISE FOR THE JEDI AS WELL...
VRRIP
SNAPT
AS ZAM AND ANAKIN STRUGGLE OVER THE BLASTER, IT GOES OFF...
...WITH UNEXPECTED RESULTS!
FTOOM
DISABLED, ZAM'S SPEEDER GOES INTO A DIVE...
...WITH OBI-WAN IN CLOSE PURSUIT.
FOOM

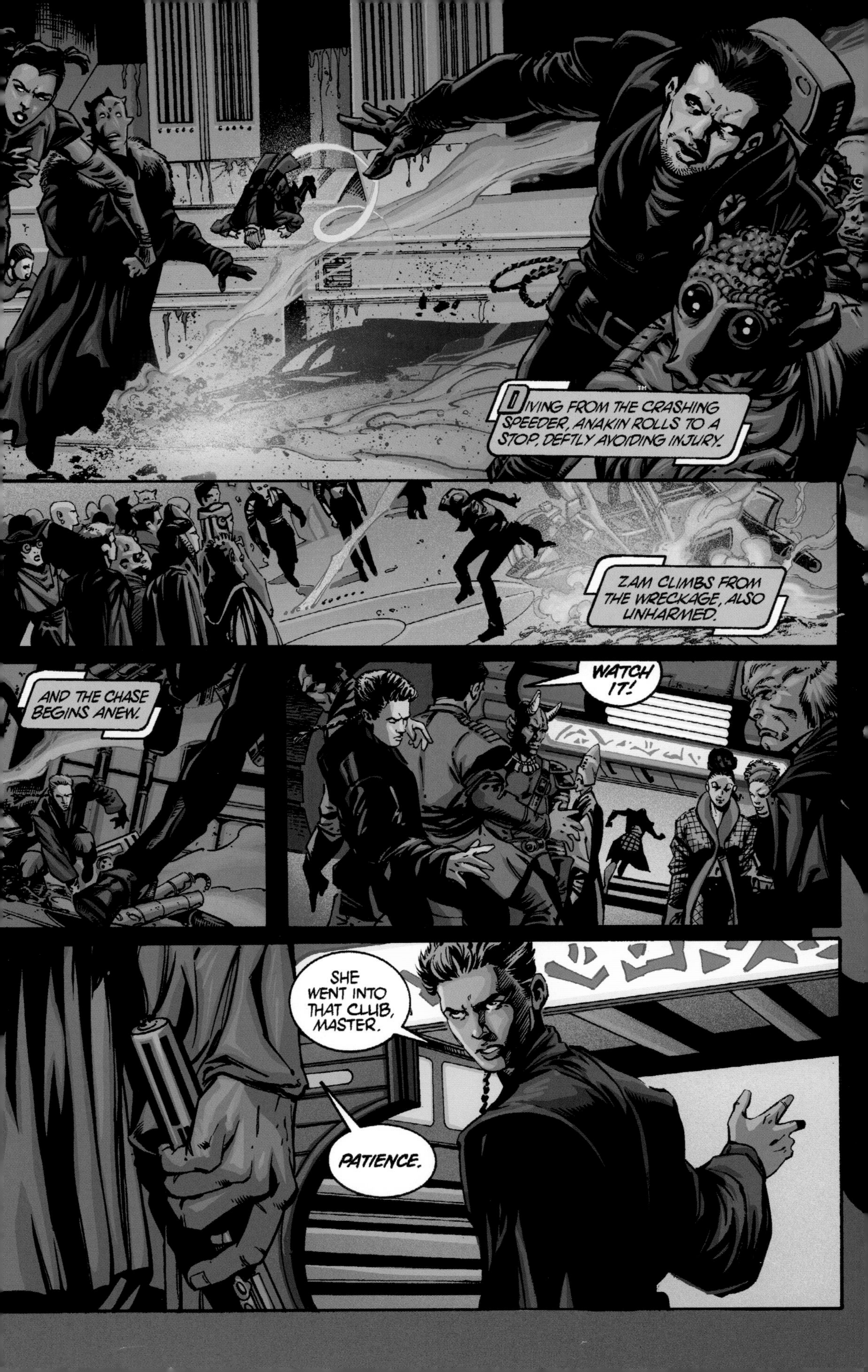

DIVING FROM THE CRASHING SPEEDER, ANAKIN ROLLS TO A STOP, DEFTLY AVOIDING INJURY.
ZAM CLIMBS FROM THE WRECKAGE, ALSO UNHARMED.
AND THE CHASE BEGINS ANEW.
WATCH IT!
SHE WENT INTO THAT CLUB, MASTER.
PATIENCE.

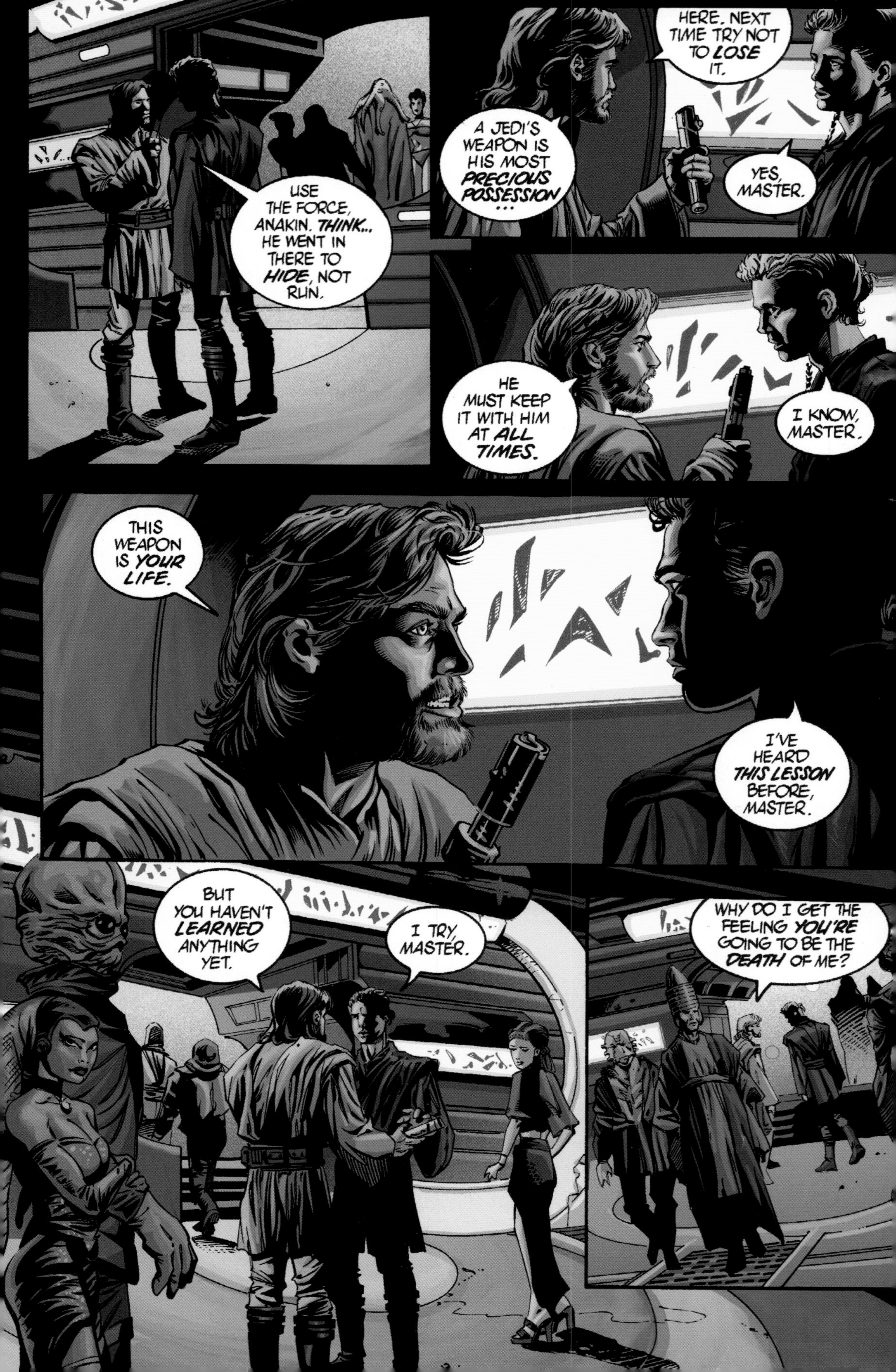
USE THE FORCE, ANAKIN. *THINK...* HE WENT IN THERE TO *HIDE*, NOT RUN.
HERE. NEXT TIME TRY NOT TO *LOSE* IT.
A JEDI'S WEAPON IS HIS MOST *PRECIOUS POSSESSION*...
YES, MASTER.
HE MUST KEEP IT WITH HIM AT *ALL TIMES*.
I KNOW, MASTER.
THIS WEAPON IS *YOUR LIFE*.
I'VE HEARD *THIS LESSON* BEFORE, MASTER.
BUT YOU HAVEN'T *LEARNED* ANYTHING YET.
I TRY, MASTER.
WHY DO I GET THE FEELING *YOU'RE* GOING TO BE THE *DEATH* OF ME?

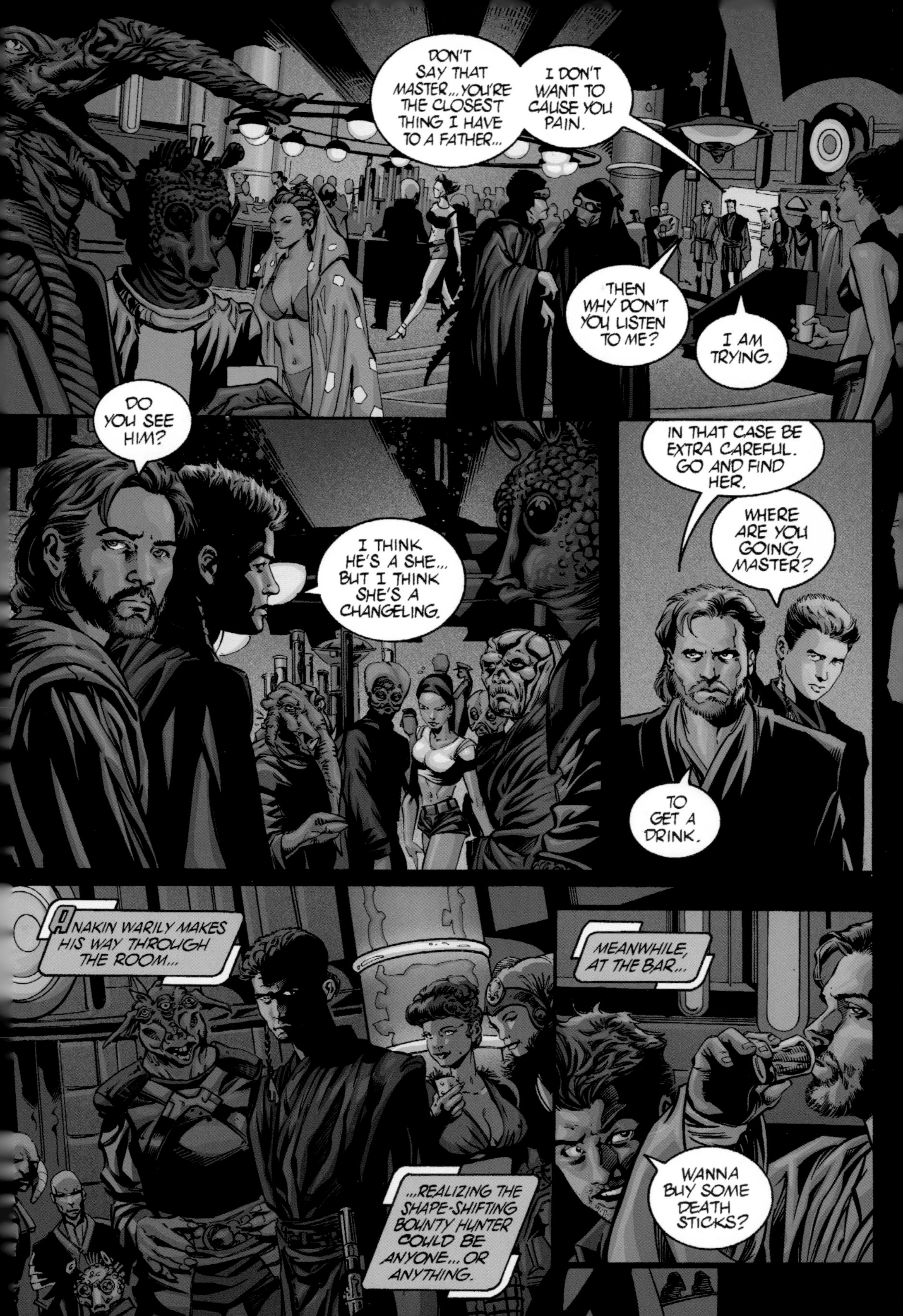
DON'T SAY THAT MASTER... YOU'RE THE CLOSEST THING I HAVE TO A FATHER...
I DON'T WANT TO CAUSE YOU PAIN.
THEN WHY DON'T YOU LISTEN TO ME?
I AM TRYING.
DO YOU SEE HIM?
I THINK HE'S A SHE... BUT I THINK SHE'S A CHANGELING.
IN THAT CASE BE EXTRA CAREFUL. GO AND FIND HER.
WHERE ARE YOU GOING, MASTER?
TO GET A DRINK.
ANAKIN WARILY MAKES HIS WAY THROUGH THE ROOM...
...REALIZING THE SHAPE-SHIFTING BOUNTY HUNTER COULD BE ANYONE... OR ANYTHING.
MEANWHILE, AT THE BAR...
WANNA BUY SOME DEATH STICKS?

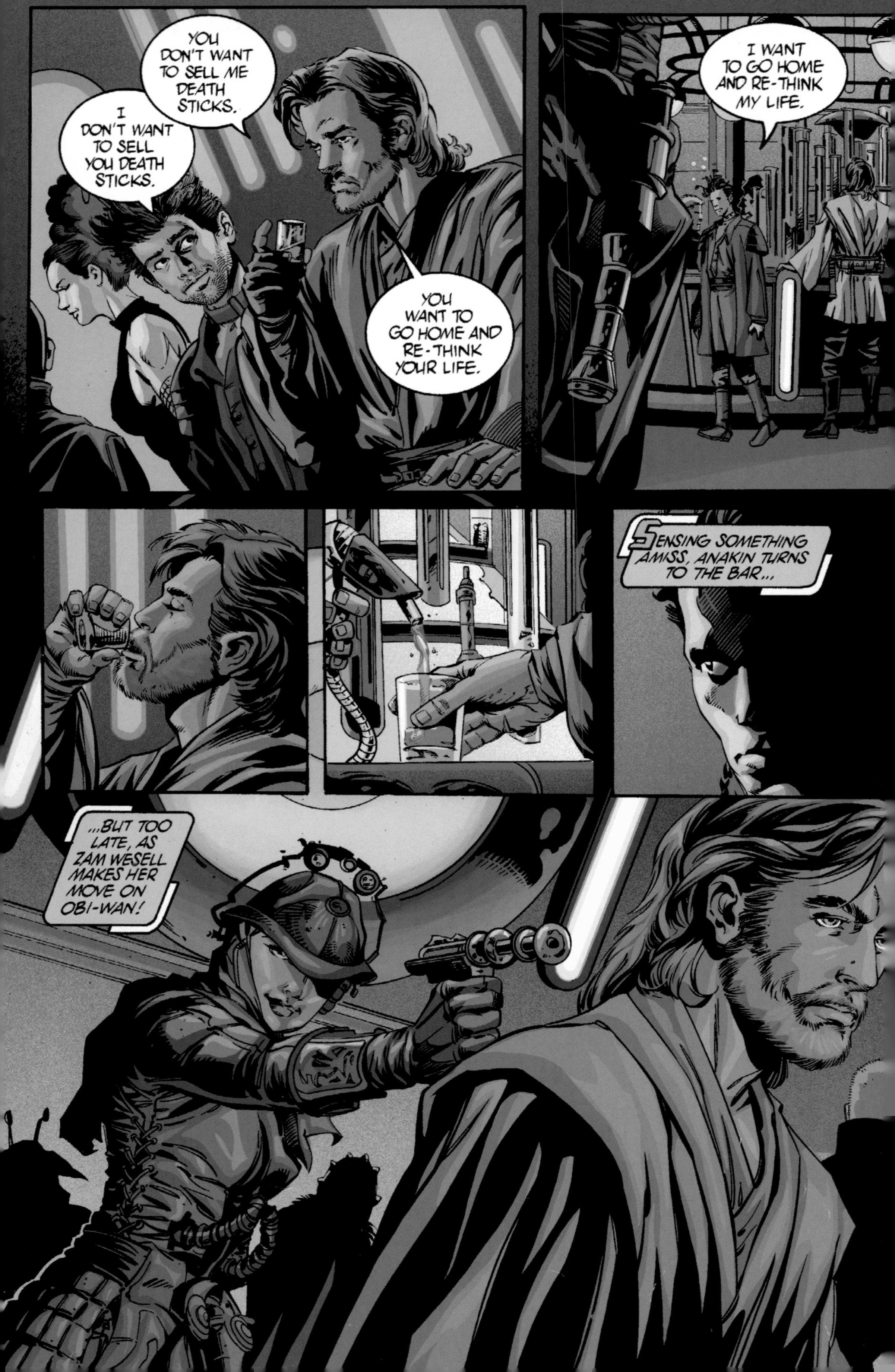
YOU DON'T WANT TO SELL ME DEATH STICKS.
I DON'T WANT TO SELL YOU DEATH STICKS.
YOU WANT TO GO HOME AND RE-THINK YOUR LIFE.
I WANT TO GO HOME AND RE-THINK MY LIFE.
SENSING SOMETHING AMISS, ANAKIN TURNS TO THE BAR...
...BUT TOO LATE, AS ZAM WESELL MAKES HER MOVE ON OBI-WAN!

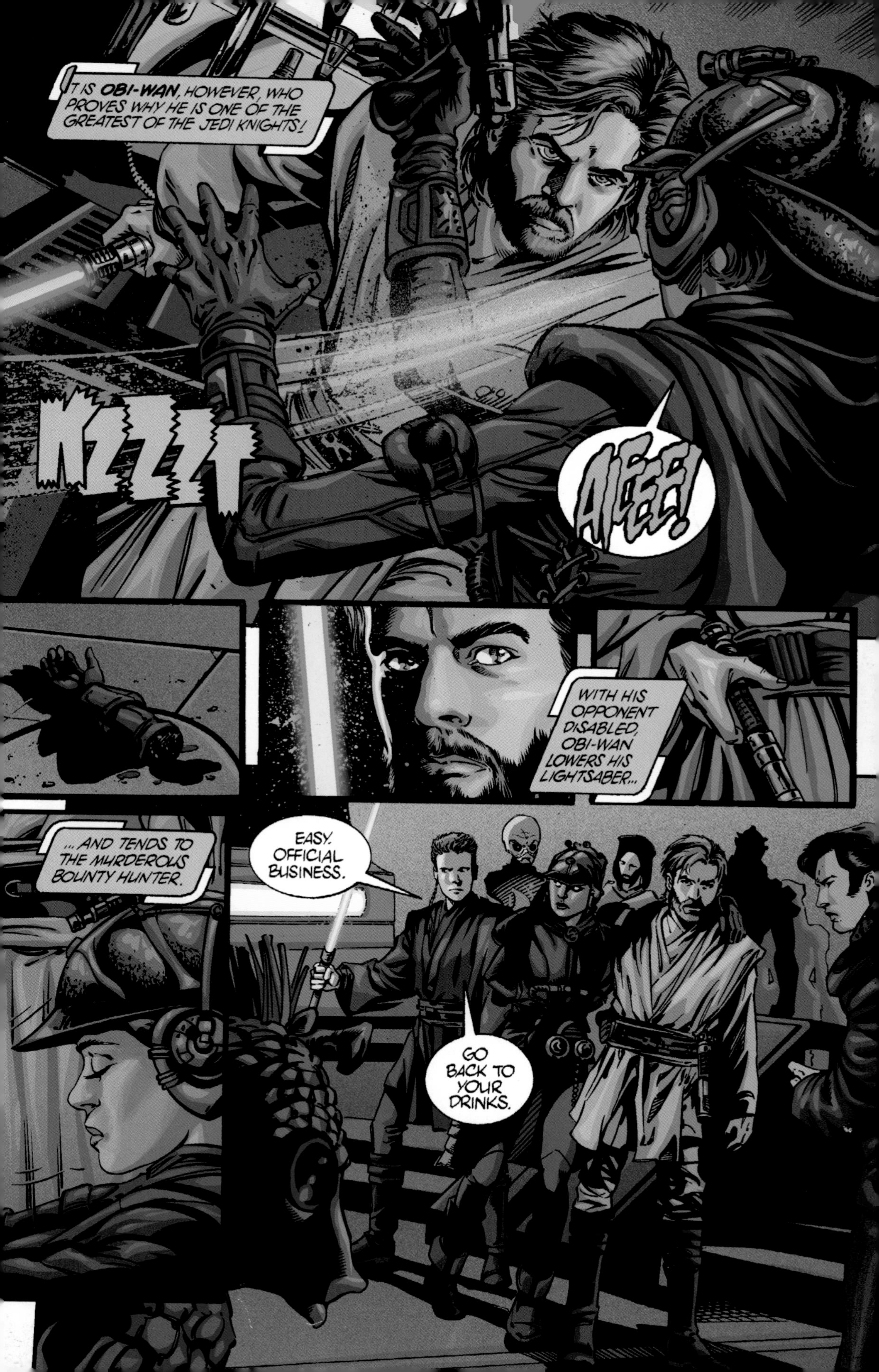
IT IS OBI-WAN, HOWEVER, WHO PROVES WHY HE IS ONE OF THE GREATEST OF THE JEDI KNIGHTS!
KZZT
AIEEE!
WITH HIS OPPONENT DISABLED, OBI-WAN LOWERS HIS LIGHTSABER...
...AND TENDS TO THE MURDEROUS BOUNTY HUNTER.
EASY. OFFICIAL BUSINESS.
GO BACK TO YOUR DRINKS.

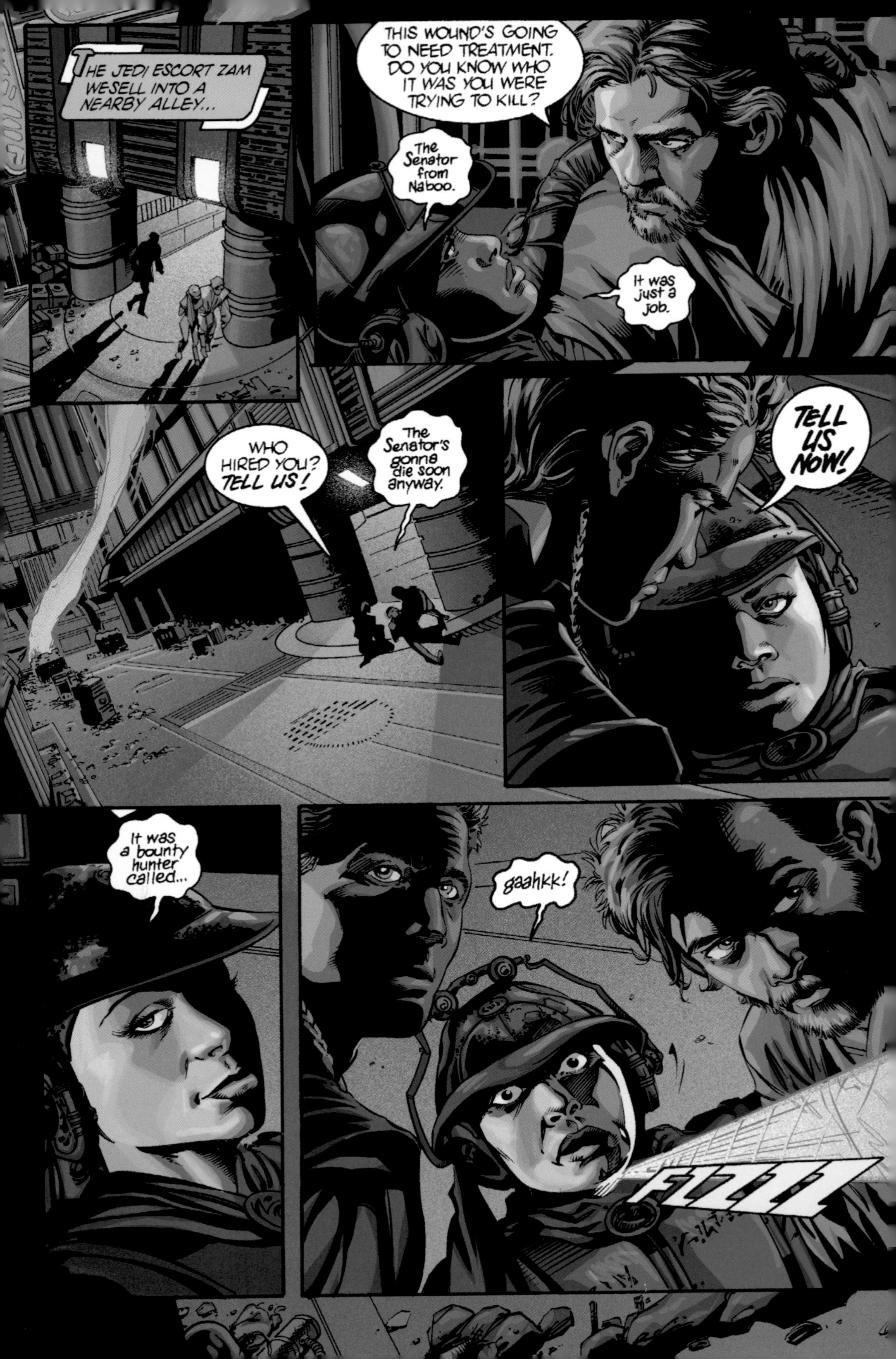
THE JEDI ESCORT ZAM WESELL INTO A NEARBY ALLEY...
THIS WOUND'S GOING TO NEED TREATMENT. DO YOU KNOW WHO IT WAS YOU WERE TRYING TO KILL?
The Senator from Naboo.
It was just a job.
WHO HIRED YOU? TELL US!
The Senator's gonna die soon anyway.
TELL US NOW!
It was a bounty hunter called...
gaahkk!
FZZT

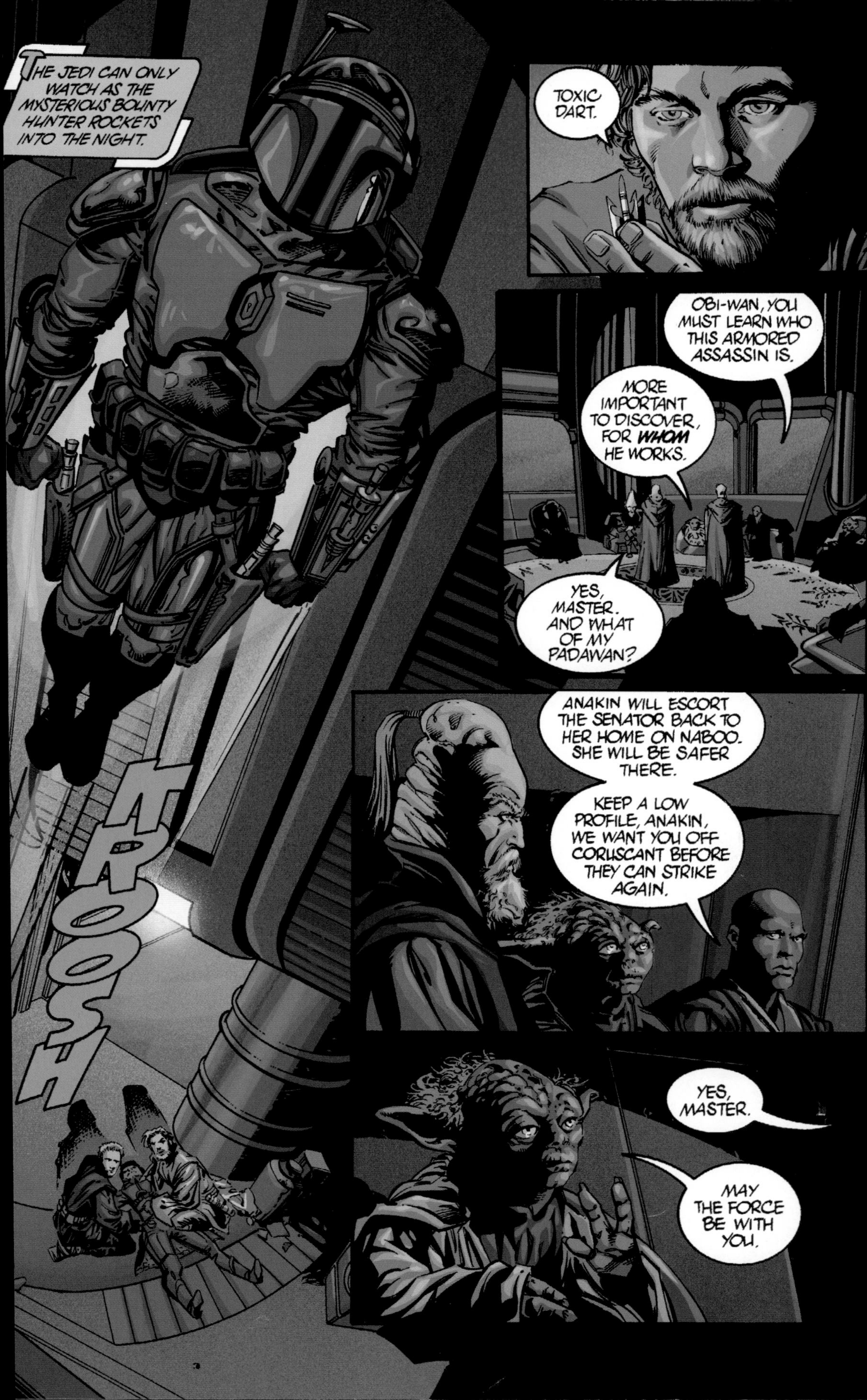
THE JEDI CAN ONLY WATCH AS THE MYSTERIOUS BOUNTY HUNTER ROCKETS INTO THE NIGHT.
KROOOSH
TOXIC DART.
OBI-WAN, YOU MUST LEARN WHO THIS ARMORED ASSASSIN IS.
MORE IMPORTANT TO DISCOVER, FOR *WHOM* HE WORKS.
YES, MASTER. AND WHAT OF MY PADAWAN?
ANAKIN WILL ESCORT THE SENATOR BACK TO HER HOME ON NABOO. SHE WILL BE SAFER THERE.
KEEP A LOW PROFILE, ANAKIN, WE WANT YOU OFF CORUSCANT BEFORE THEY CAN STRIKE AGAIN.
YES, MASTER.
MAY THE FORCE BE WITH YOU.

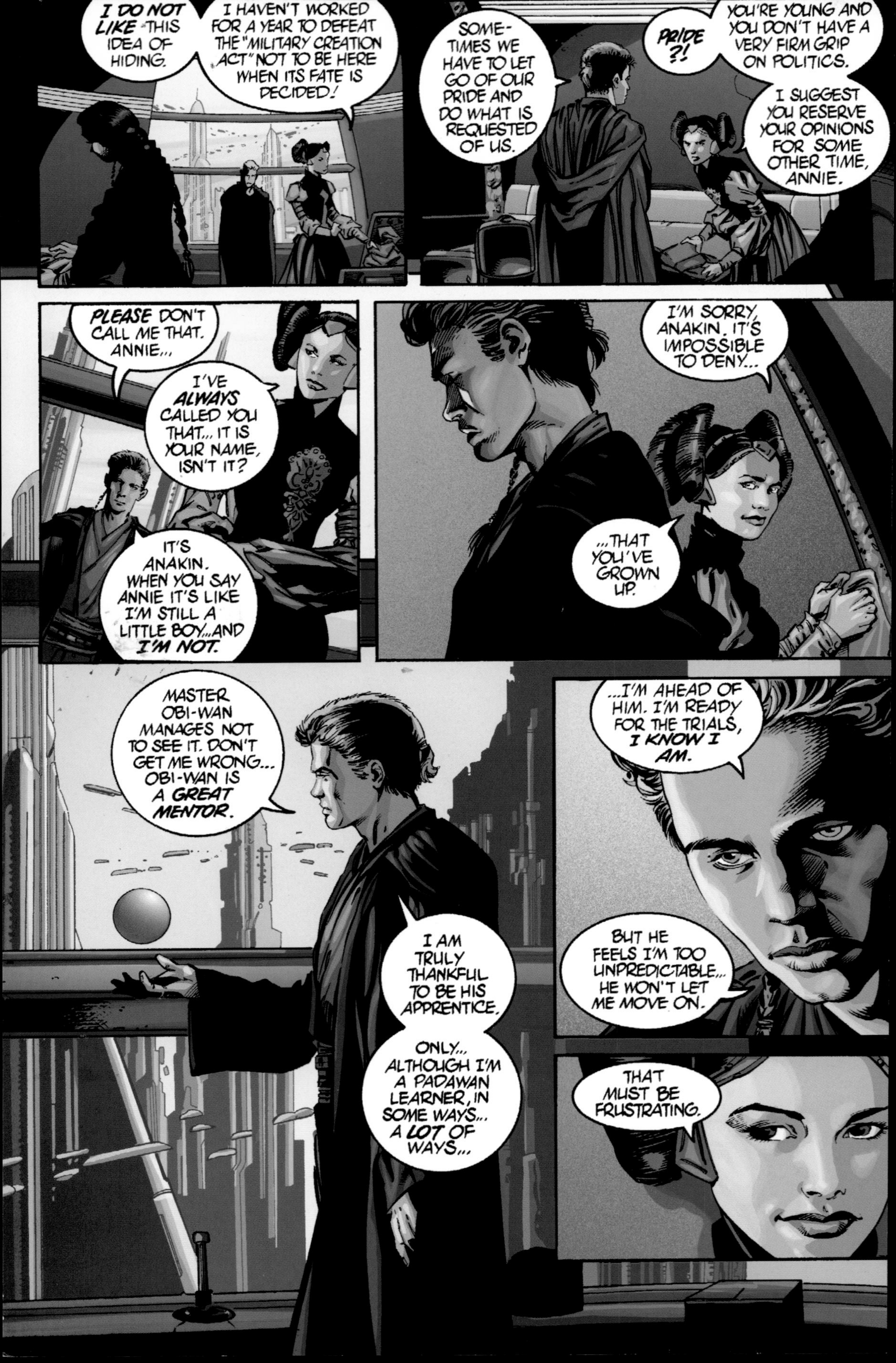

I DO NOT LIKE THIS IDEA OF HIDING.
I HAVEN'T WORKED FOR A YEAR TO DEFEAT THE "MILITARY CREATION ACT" NOT TO BE HERE WHEN ITS FATE IS DECIDED!
SOME-TIMES WE HAVE TO LET GO OF OUR PRIDE AND DO WHAT IS REQUESTED OF US.
PRIDE?!
YOU'RE YOUNG AND YOU DON'T HAVE A VERY FIRM GRIP ON POLITICS.
I SUGGEST YOU RESERVE YOUR OPINIONS FOR SOME OTHER TIME, ANNIE.
PLEASE DON'T CALL ME THAT. ANNIE...
I'VE ALWAYS CALLED YOU THAT... IT IS YOUR NAME, ISN'T IT?
IT'S ANAKIN. WHEN YOU SAY ANNIE IT'S LIKE I'M STILL A LITTLE BOY...AND I'M NOT.
I'M SORRY, ANAKIN. IT'S IMPOSSIBLE TO DENY...
...THAT YOU'VE GROWN UP.
MASTER OBI-WAN MANAGES NOT TO SEE IT. DON'T GET ME WRONG... OBI-WAN IS A GREAT MENTOR.
I AM TRULY THANKFUL TO BE HIS APPRENTICE.
ONLY... ALTHOUGH I'M A PADAWAN LEARNER, IN SOME WAYS... A LOT OF WAYS...
...I'M AHEAD OF HIM. I'M READY FOR THE TRIALS, I KNOW I AM.
BUT HE FEELS I'M TOO UNPREDICTABLE... HE WON'T LET ME MOVE ON.
THAT MUST BE FRUSTRATING.

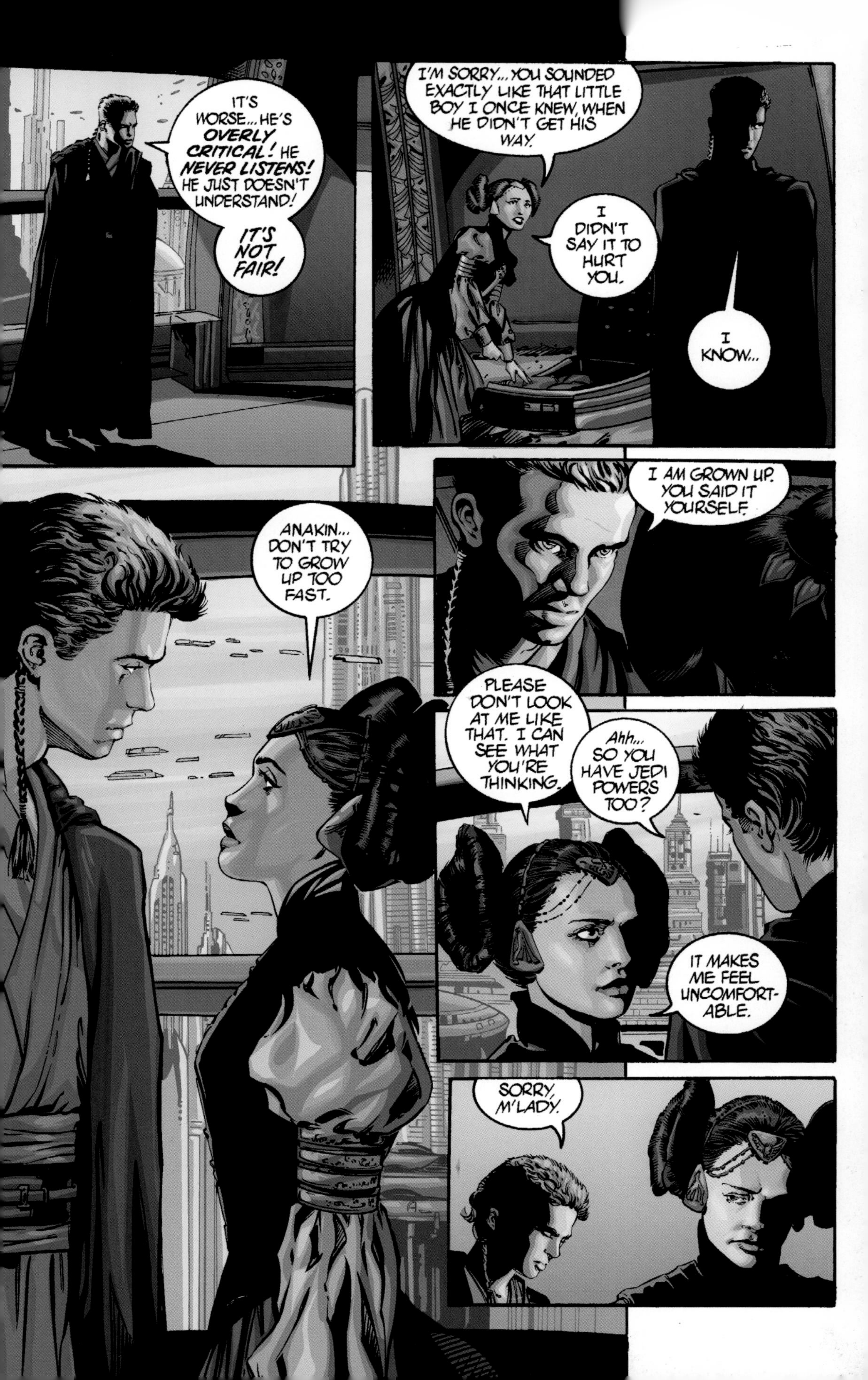
IT'S WORSE... HE'S OVERLY CRITICAL! HE NEVER LISTENS! HE JUST DOESN'T UNDERSTAND!
IT'S NOT FAIR!
I'M SORRY... YOU SOUNDED EXACTLY LIKE THAT LITTLE BOY I ONCE KNEW, WHEN HE DIDN'T GET HIS WAY.
I DIDN'T SAY IT TO HURT YOU.
I KNOW...
ANAKIN... DON'T TRY TO GROW UP TOO FAST.
I AM GROWN UP. YOU SAID IT YOURSELF.
PLEASE DON'T LOOK AT ME LIKE THAT. I CAN SEE WHAT YOU'RE THINKING.
Ahh... SO YOU HAVE JEDI POWERS TOO?
IT MAKES ME FEEL UNCOMFORT-ABLE.
SORRY, M'LADY.

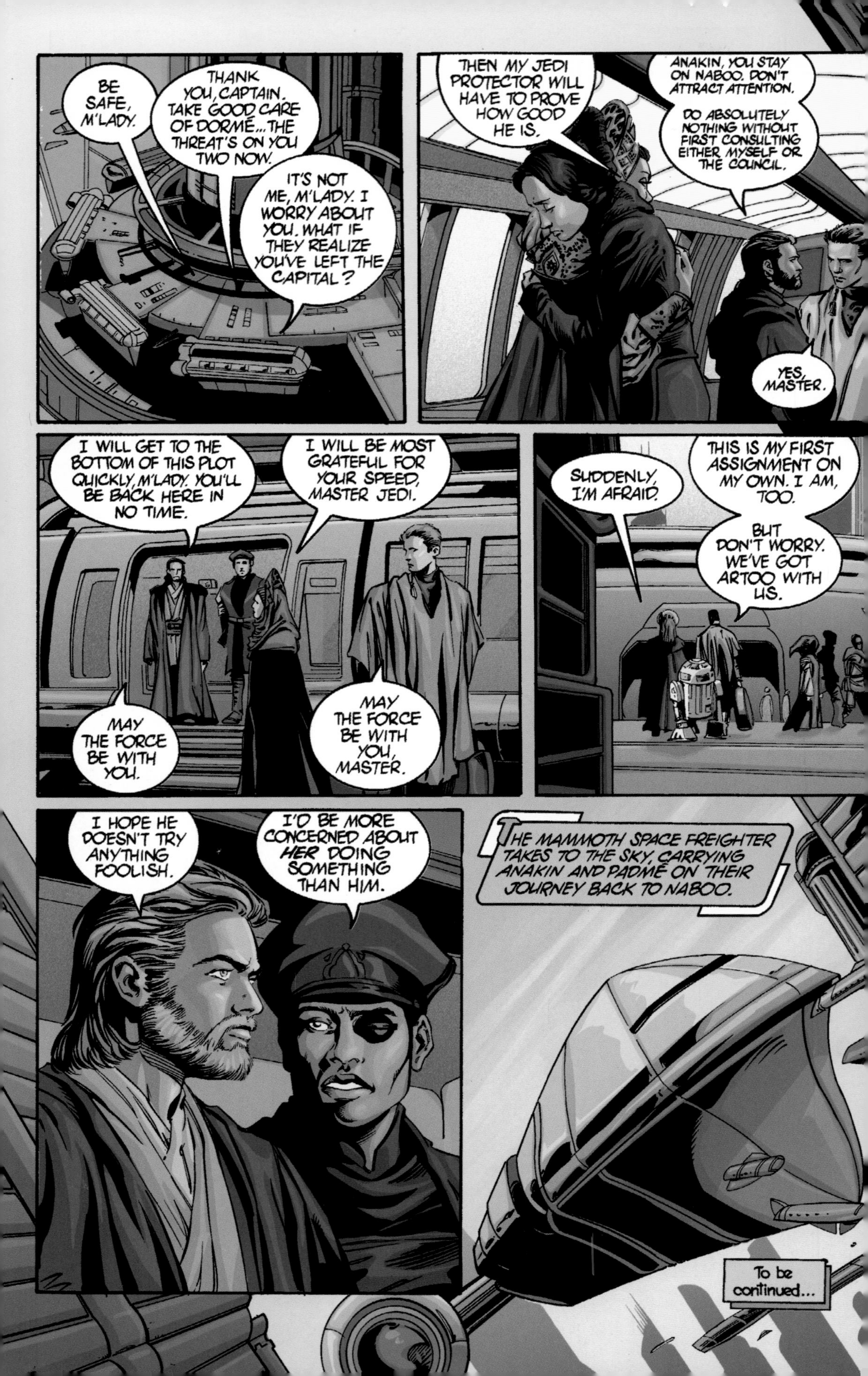
BE SAFE, M'LADY.
THANK YOU, CAPTAIN. TAKE GOOD CARE OF DORMÉ... THE THREAT'S ON YOU TWO NOW.
IT'S NOT ME, M'LADY. I WORRY ABOUT YOU. WHAT IF THEY REALIZE YOU'VE LEFT THE CAPITAL?
THEN MY JEDI PROTECTOR WILL HAVE TO PROVE HOW GOOD HE IS.
ANAKIN, YOU STAY ON NABOO. DON'T ATTRACT ATTENTION.
DO ABSOLUTELY NOTHING WITHOUT FIRST CONSULTING EITHER MYSELF OR THE COUNCIL.
YES, MASTER.
I WILL GET TO THE BOTTOM OF THIS PLOT QUICKLY, M'LADY. YOU'LL BE BACK HERE IN NO TIME.
I WILL BE MOST GRATEFUL FOR YOUR SPEED, MASTER JEDI.
MAY THE FORCE BE WITH YOU.
MAY THE FORCE BE WITH YOU, MASTER.
SUDDENLY, I'M AFRAID.
THIS IS MY FIRST ASSIGNMENT ON MY OWN. I AM, TOO.
BUT DON'T WORRY. WE'VE GOT ARTOO WITH US.
I HOPE HE DOESN'T TRY ANYTHING FOOLISH.
I'D BE MORE CONCERNED ABOUT HER DOING SOMETHING THAN HIM.
THE MAMMOTH SPACE FREIGHTER TAKES TO THE SKY, CARRYING ANAKIN AND PADMÉ ON THEIR JOURNEY BACK TO NABOO.
To be continued...

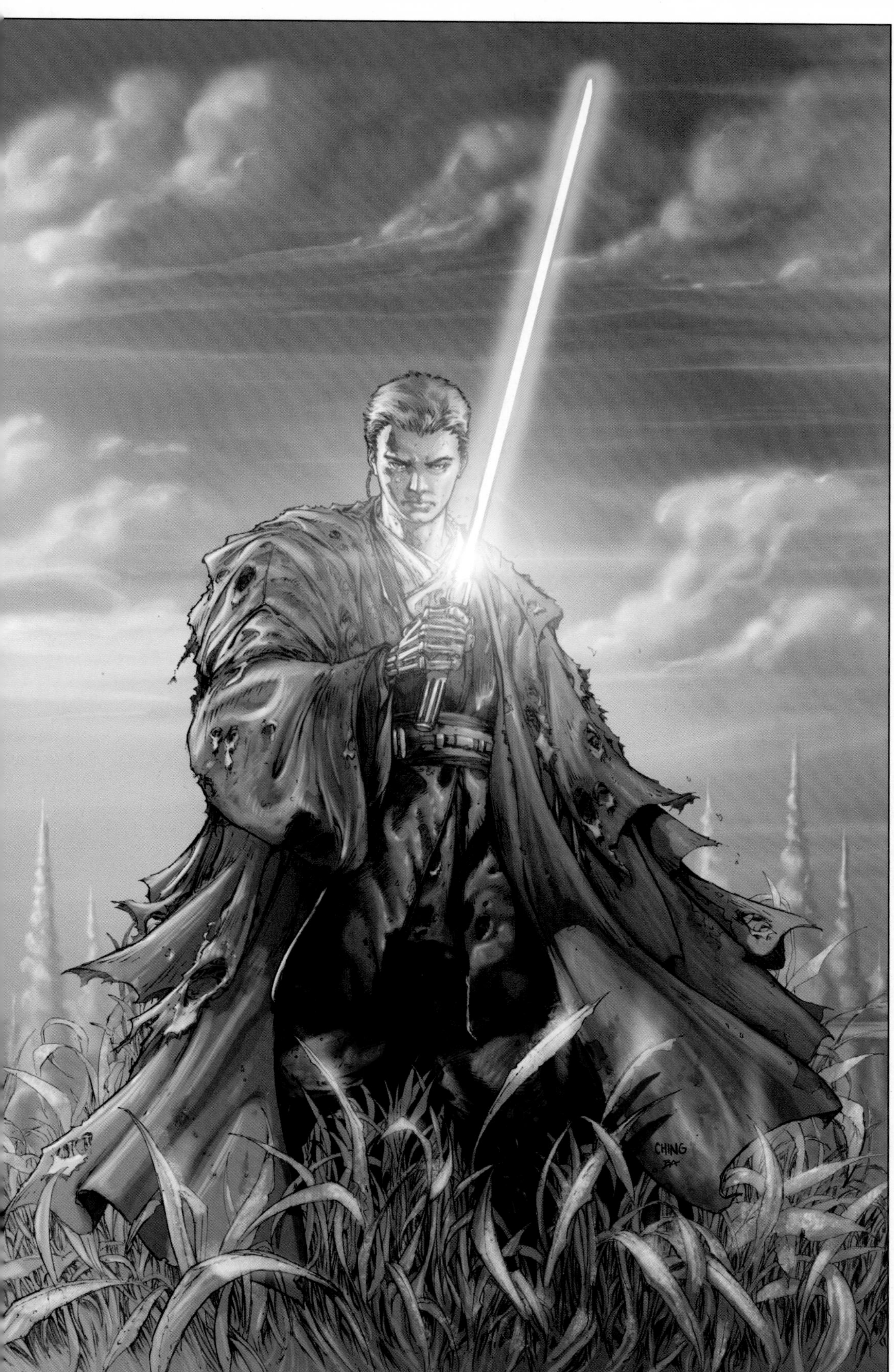
CHING
BA

PENCILS BY **BRIAN CHING**
COLORS BY **BRAD ANDERSON**

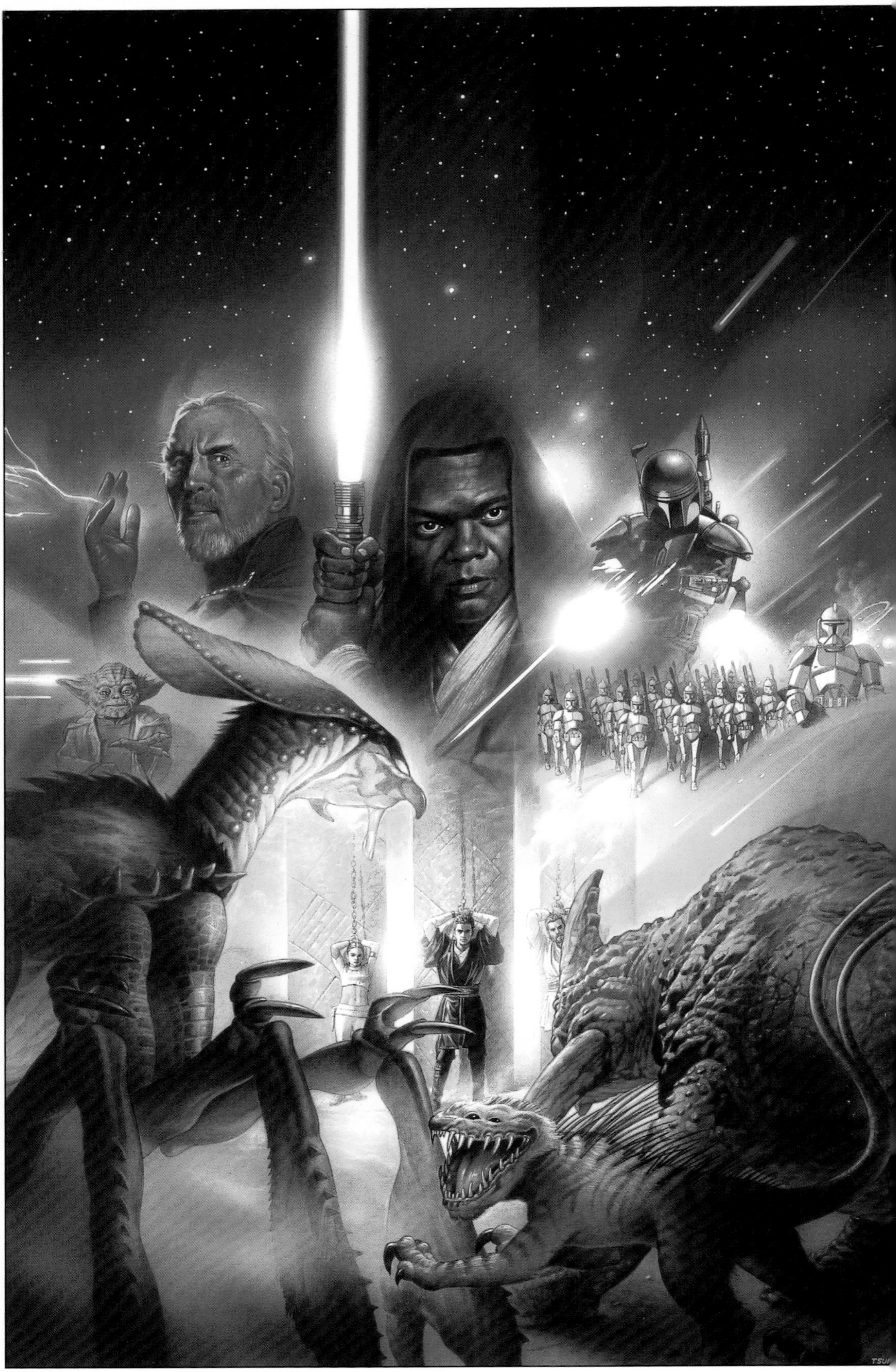
TSUI

ART BY **TSUNEO SANDA**